Halfmoon Confidential

Also by Edward Fotheringill

Previous Volumes of the *Wisdom Trilogy*:

**Lanterns in the Mist
Darkness Withdrawn OR The Eclipse of
Nietzsche's Shadow**

Halfmoon Confidential

Edward Fotheringill

Booklocker.com
2008

Author's Note

Halfmoon Confidential is a work of fiction. The village of Halfmoon and all of the characters portrayed are purely imaginary.

A profound debt of gratitude is owed to the scholarship of John Dobson, from whom the theory of apparitional causation and its tangential scientific pronouncements have been borrowed. Any errors in or misrepresentation of the theory are my responsibility.

All places and times are pretty much the same: the demands of human nature cannot be satisfied by nature itself. There is an insidious disconnect between the hopes and dreams of the human mind and the brute facts of human existence. This disconnect creates an inscrutable maze where death looms as a finality which cannot be effectively processed or negotiated by human consciousness.

Don't think for a minute that death means you've crossed over to the other side. That's an easy way of disposing of the problem. No, death can live right here within the earthly realm. You can see it in people's eyes. That's where death hovers.

Some elderly folks harbor the presence of death in their eyes. They sit crooked in their porch chairs and look out at you through faces sallow and drawn, glassy eyes frozen in milky gray obscurity. There's no life in their eyes. Just a stone-quiet paralysis. A paralysis born of seeing and feeling and thinking too much. Seeing and feeling and thinking too much about life's desperations. There's a point where the illusory hopes and dreams that have kept them going just curl up and die. That's when it happens. Death. The mechanisms of the body continue to bump along. Nothing glorified about it. But down deep, somewhere behind the glassy eyes, is that stone-quiet paralysis. No desire lurks there. No fear. No hope. Nothing.

But it's not only the elderly who see through death's eyes. Some people are born that way. These people come into the world under a bad moon where hopes and dreams are stillborn. When you look into their eyes, you see a soulless void. Dead to begin with, they burden the world with destruction and chaos. They are ministers of evil. God bless and keep you if they ever cross your path.

Then there are those rare few who are blessed with some kind of holy prescience. These few die unto life in order to be reborn. This dying unto life can come in only one way: cheating the genetic programming away from the fulfillment of biological necessities and toward the realization of spiritual ones. Death is in the eyes of the enlightened. No doubt about it. But there is a difference. The death in their eyes is bigger than life. More expansive. Downright infinite.

Chapter 1

High on a wooded hillside in Halfmoon, Vermont, in a dense grove of tall white poplars, a bald eagle majestically sits atop the highest of the poplar crowns. It slowly rotates its regal, white head, surveying the earthly realm with prescient circumspection. The large, predatory bird would be considered an incongruous presence, for it is calculated to be endangered in these parts. But incongruous presences haunt Halfmoon and its environs. Shortly, they will make themselves known. And it will seem as if the forces of nature had converged on the innocent like a macabre maelstrom of unwarranted strife.

The bright yellow irises of the bald eagle's eyes shine in recognition of a human form moving about in a clearing below. The weathered aviator cocks its head, its curved, yellow bill pointing toward the red western sky like a cipher of doom. In a moment's flash, the bird opens its solid brown-feathered chest and spreads its mighty wings to a full span of seven feet. In this ominous posture, summoning ancient presences of prehistoric wanderings, it witnesses the human form with some distant and mysterious recollection of pity.

~ ~ ~ ~ ~

Alexander Lessing jumped into his Dodge Ram pickup, slammed the gear into DRIVE, and sped off a little too fast down the long, precipitous, dirt driveway toward Snake Hollow Road. It wasn't as if he had to be somewhere in a hurry. It was just that he was excited. He had made up his mind. Finally.

Alexander slowed down a bit at the end of the driveway and turned left onto Snake Hollow. The truck fishtailed on the turn, but he paid it no mind. After all, he was excited. Taking it up to fifty-five miles per hour on the narrow, backcountry road, he zoomed past two dilapidated farmhouses sitting back off the roadside some thirty yards and an old trailer founded just behind the forest tree line. Long-time Vermonters lived in those dwellings. Alexander didn't see them much, but they were there. A couple of old widows and a retired New York City homicide cop. Yeah, they were there. Somewhere.

Bearing right onto Riverneck Road, Alexander crossed over the Ottaquechee River on the Riverneck Bridge. As he navigated the wooden span, the sun was setting in the autumn sky, reflecting orange and red off the lazy current of the rock-speckled river. An eighth of a mile later, he turned left onto Route 4 and headed for the Elk Head Saloon. That's where he liked to be. That's where he could be himself. Whoever that was.

Chapter 2

"So, would you like to talk about it?"

"No. Honestly, what good would that do?"

"Well, Raymond, that is why we get together for these sessions. To talk."

"Doc, you know me. I'm not a troublemaker. I've pretty much gone along with the program, haven't I? I've babbled on about myself and my afflictions for two years now."

"Yes, Raymond, it's been about two years."

"And I'm tired of talking. Tired of dwelling on myself. I don't want to know any more about myself."

"Well, that's not a very healthy attitude, is it?"

"To me, it's completely healthy. To me, it's a sign that I'm ready to look outside myself. That I'm ready to consider the bigger picture."

"The bigger picture? What bigger picture?"

"Life. That's the bigger picture. There is life outside the walls of Sheppard Pratt. Did you know that?"

"Now, Raymond. There's no reason to be hostile."

"Hostile? I'm not being hostile. I'm just saying that there is life out there. Outside of me. It's every bit as important as I am. I'm just saying that I'm ready to go and see what it's all about. I'm ready to contribute to it, become part of it."

"Well, Raymond, I think you should let me be the judge of that."

"Well, I'm trying to tell you that I'm ready. I can make it this time. Really."

"I'm sorry, Raymond. The clock on my desk tells me our time is up. Enjoy your weekend."

"But, Doc. Don't you hear what I'm saying? I want to live my life. I want to connect with the world. Is that an unreasonable request?"

"Raymond, we can talk about this next week. I really must be going. I have an engagement."

"That's my very point, Doc. That's it. You're going out into the world. You have an engagement with life. See how healthy that is? That's what I want to do. I just want to lead a normal life. Does that sound crazy to you?"

"Raymond, you know we don't use that word here."

"What word? 'Crazy'? I don't see anything wrong with that word. People do crazy things. That's why they land in here with you."

Chapter 3

Alexander Lessing sipped contemplatively on his third pint of Smuttynose Old Brown Dog Ale. The predominately hopped ale reminded him of the bitter he had so enjoyed during his university days at Oxford. *Those were the days. Sitting in the dark shadows of noisy pubs, drinking beer with scholars brandishing large, sloping foreheads and receding hairlines. Conversing about the dimensions of moral experience in Plato and Aristotle, Augustine and Aquinas, Kant and Hegel. Those were the days...*

"You seem quiet tonight, Alex."

Alex raised his head and looked into the wide, brown eyes of Madeline Kerr, the barmaid at the Elk Head Saloon. Madeline was forty-something. A Vermont girl through and through. Grew up down the road near White River Junction. Orphaned at age seven when her parents died in a freak hunting accident. Raised by her grandparents on a dairy farm. Alex considered her wiry, beguiling frame, her full breasts beneath her navy blue crewneck sweater, her mischievous oval face with a peaches-and-cream complexion and a scattering of brown freckles meandering across her nose from one cheek to the other. Alex wondered if she had freckles on her bountiful breasts. "Oh, I'm just doing some thinking."

"What about?"

Alex leaned forward, bracing himself on the bar with his elbows. "I've made a decision. It feels good when that happens."

Madeline smiled and nodded in agreement. "So what have you decided?"

"I've decided to leave the university. I'm going to quit!" Alex peered into his beer glass and contemplated the brown ale's frothy head. "I've never quit a job in my entire life. It feels good to be decisive. To say *no* when things no longer make sense."

"I always thought you enjoyed teaching."

"Oh, I have. Don't get me wrong—it's been a great ride. But now, everything has a nasty political odor. What the administration calls political correctness, I call intellectual dishonesty. Today, teaching is more about coddling the students than it is about communicating the seminal ideas that have shaped the movements of Western culture." Alex leaned back and shrugged his shoulders. "Anyway, I'm quitting."

Aaron Riley turned his big, burly head to the right and peered out from under the brim of his red Budweiser Beer ball cap. "I couldn't help overhearin', Alex. So you're quittin' your job? Nothin' wrong with that. I've pretty much quit every job I ever had. It's not good to let grass grow under your feet. Especially if the grass doesn't suit you. No, sir. Gotta keep on movin'."

Alex surveyed the massive torso of Aaron Riley and pondered the remark. Then he pondered the source of the remark. Aaron Riley. A great hulk of a man. Six-feet-three, two hundred fifty-five pounds. Juvenile delinquent at the age of sixteen. Stole cars in high school and set them on fire. Why? Because he liked to. Spent two years in a juvenile correction facility. When he was eighteen, he disappeared. No one in these parts knows where he was. And Aaron never said, either. At the age of twenty-five, he reappeared in Halfmoon. He had changed. Really. He was a good man. Why? No one knows. And Aaron hasn't pontificated on it, either. Now, he's fifty-five. Lives alone in a log cabin on a dirt road off Route 4 on the outskirts of Halfmoon. Fixes truck transmissions for a living. When will he quit that job? Who knows?

"Aaron, I'm just tired of all the bullshit. You know what I mean?"

"Yes, sir. I do."

Madeline pulled two more pints of Smuttynose and slid the brimming glasses in front of the interlocutors. "On the house, gentlemen." She winked and sashayed down to the other end of the bar in response to a crowd of thirsty patrons.

Alex watched Madeline's alluring hips sway to and fro as she strode away. He raised his eyebrows at Aaron.

"Oh, yeah. I get your drift."

Alex nodded knowingly. "Anyway, I'm going to quit. Think I'll do some traveling."

"Hmmm. Where you gonna go?"

Alex considered the question. "Don't know. Some place where I can find myself."

Aaron shook his head and groaned. "Jesus Christ! You talk about how you want to get away from all the bullshit, and then you tell me you want to go on some fuckin' odyssey in search of yourself." Aaron shifted his bulky frame on the barstool. "You just have no clue, do you? All those philosophy books you've read. They don't help much in real life, do they? Alex, the simple truth is this: If your mind is all fucked up, it doesn't matter where you go. Your fucked-up mind is gonna go with you."

Alex shrugged and looked forlornly into his glass of creamy brown nectar. He felt his mind spinning down into a dark chasm where personal demons might very well exist. "Well, I've got to do something."

Unconvinced, Aaron shook his head. "Change of subject. How's Ray doin'?"

Alex felt a bolt of dizziness cascade through his temples. He inhaled deeply. "That's another thing I've got to get some closure on."

Chapter 4

October 8, 2000

Dear Ray,

I'm writing from the farm in Halfmoon. Fall is underway and as majestic as ever. There's something about the movement of the seasons that beckons the soul. Today, a range and mixture in the colors of the leaves and a coolness in the air exhilarate the senses. But, lo, another hard winter approaches. The crunch of the earth beneath one's feet betrays this.

*I guess you're wondering why I'm here and not at the university. I've decided to take my long-overdue sabbatical. I've been relieved of my teaching duties for the next year (with full pay!) under the guise of writing a book on ethics. What I have not revealed to my chair, or to the administration at large, is that I'm not coming back. I just don't need it anymore! Do you know what the chair of philosophy said to me the last time we were preparing course offerings? He said, "Alex, things have changed. Rather than offer what **we** think is necessary for the budding young minds, we will offer what **they** think is necessary. We've got to fill the classes, increase enrollment, make the Board of Regents happy." What's happened to provocative education, you ask? It's a thing of the past. Just show me the money!*

Luckily, the house in Baltimore is paid off, as well as the Vermont farm. But on to more important matters: how are you? The last time I came to visit you (has it been two years already?), you were sedated to the point where we could not carry on a conversation.

To this day, Ray, I don't know what drove you over the edge. I mean, I have my suspicions as to the contributing factors. But I really won't understand what happened until I hear it from you. Damn, I miss our conversations! I also miss drinking with you, although I fear (nay, I know!) that alcohol is one of the personal demons that has landed you in Sheppard Pratt.

A few weeks ago, I had lunch at Harvard with our old friend Harvey Blackstone. I dare say I'm concerned about Harvey's weight. I guess we all have our afflictions. At any rate, I informed him of your situation. Never at a loss for words, he had some rather interesting comments, which I will try to recount to you verbatim. Harvey said the following:

"I'm not at all surprised. Raymond is a tragic flaw in the cosmos. His story begins with such fanfare and promise as he takes his Ph.D. in physics from Cal Tech, with highest honors. But then the worm begins to turn. For some reason, he can find work only at Kent State, teaching Introduction to Physics. Here we have a brilliant mind, poised to make a contribution, and the forces of the cosmos leave him in a state of mental atrophy. After five years of intellectual humiliation, Raymond quits physics and becomes a carpet salesman for Sears and Roebuck. Raymond, a carpet salesman! A cosmic mistake if ever there was one. But was it a mistake? That's the interesting question. We mortals may deem it so. Shakespeare, on the other hand, would disagree. That grand sage of letters understood that

tragedy is destined to some, no less than joy. With joy, we do not try to understand its descent upon us. Why disturb the joy with some herculean effort of the intellect? With tragedy, we try to understand but cannot. Enduring tragedy without understanding may, in fact, be the greatest test that life administers."

Harvey's take on your difficult situation is sobering to say the least.

Well, dear brother, I must close for now. Please write if you're up to it.

Yours,
Alexander

Chapter 5

On a wooden bench under a majestic oak tree, Raymond Lessing sat in the common area outside Building B on the Towson campus of the Sheppard Pratt Hospital. The fall air was cool on his face, and the salient aroma of dead leaves tickled his nostrils with every breath. Acorns plummeted from the branches above him with precise regularity. The squirrels were up to no good. Raymond cast his glance at a single white cloud floating aimlessly across the vastness of the crystal blue sky. *The cloud is like an evanescent electron roaming in the atom of the sky. Here one moment, gone the next.* An acorn tumbled down from above, not without force, and whacked him on the left kneecap. Raymond winced with pain but then smiled. *Gravity. We are condemned to be earthbound.* Raymond stretched his legs out in front of him, crossed his left shoe over his right, and put his hands behind his head, elbows splayed out in relaxed repose. His mind was coming back to him. Slowly but surely, it was coming back. He smiled knowingly. He had been deep-sixing his Aripiprazole for the last month. No one was the wiser. No one but he.

Chapter 6

Alice Thornberry shuffled across the maple-planked kitchen floor in her fur-lined moccasins, leaned over the dark soapstone counter next to the sink, and lifted the receiver off its wall base. "Hello? Who's there?" Alice always answered the phone this way. She wanted to know who was calling, so she didn't hesitate to ask.

"Hi, Alice. Rick Applegate here. How's everything out at your place?"

"Oh, can't complain. This time of year, the mice are lookin' for lodgin'. So I got my traps set."

"Yeah, they can be a nuisance. That's for sure."

Alice held the phone in silence. She squinted and pursed her lips expectantly.

"Look, Alice, I got some news for you. You might want to sit down. Can you do that for me?"

"Sure. Let me get my chair." Alice shuffled her creaky, arthritic, seventy-two-year-old body over to the Formica-topped kitchen table, pulled out a straight-backed, wooden chair, and eased herself down onto it. "Okay. I'm sittin' down."

"Alice, we found Jed."

"Jed? What do you mean, you found Jed?"

"I mean we found him. What's left of him."

Alice swallowed hard, her beady brown eyes darting back and forth. "Well, I don't understand. Jed's been missin' for ten years."

"Well, I know that, Alice. I know that. Let me explain, okay?"

Alice's jaw clamped down tight. "Okay," she said through clenched teeth.

"Well, this is what happened. About a mile south of you off Snake Hollow Road, up in the woods, some excavation was done. A couple from New York City had bought the land from Emma Slaughter. They're building a house. Anyway, once the trees were cleared, the contractor sent in a crew to dig the footing for the house. And, well, that's when they found Jed."

Alice rubbed her red, bulbous nose with the back of her right hand. "Go on."

"Well, there were mostly just bones. And his skull. We sent a bone fragment to the forensic lab in Burlington. We got a DNA match for Jed."

Alice reached across the kitchen table. Pulled the bottle of I.W. Harper close to her, unscrewed the cap, grasped the neck of the bottle firmly with her right hand, and took a long pull of bourbon. She winced as the burn cascaded down her esophagus and into the pit of her belly.

"Alice? You there?"

"Yeah. I'm here." Beads of perspiration glistened on Alice's narrow forehead. "How do you know it was Jed's DNA?"

"When Jed was with the Halfmoon Fire Department, they ran a DNA test. They do it for all the firefighters."

Alice stared at the bottle of I.W. Harper. Screwed the cap back on. "Well, what do I need to do?"

"Well," the sheriff faltered, "nothing at the moment. But, uh, there is something else."

Alice felt her jaw loosen up. The bourbon was doing its magic. "What else?"

"Well, we had Jed's skull examined. It looks like somebody whacked him in the head. Real hard. That's how he died. The medical examiner reckons he was hit with some kind of blunt instrument. Probably something metal."

Alice again reached for the bottle of I.W. Harper. Pulled it to her. Unscrewed the cap. "So you're sayin' somebody killed Jed? Is that what you're sayin'?"

"Yeah, Alice. That's what I'm saying."

"And somebody buried him up in the woods?"

"Yeah."

"Hmmm. So I guess you're gonna try to find out who did it. Is that what you're gonna do?"

"Yeah. That's what we're going do."

Alice slowly nodded her head up and down. "Okay then. Bye."

"Bye, Alice."

Alice Thornberry rested the receiver on the kitchen table. She knocked back a good pull of bourbon and placed the bottle beside the handset. Spreading her tired, old hands palms down, the widow considered her wrinkled skin and gnarled fingers. "Fuck me," she grumbled under her breath, as she rose to hang up the phone.

Chapter 7

October 15, 2000

Dear Alex,

Receiving your letter was a pleasant surprise. I envy your being in Vermont. Not a more beautiful place in the fall. Please forgive my choppy thoughts. They are all I have at the moment. Sometimes it literally hurts to think. But I do have some good days. Sometimes I gather myself and can see clearly. When that happens, I want to leave my cage and fly like a bird.

Tell Harvey to go shit in his hat. And for the record, selling rugs at Sears and Roebuck is no tragedy! For God's sake, what melodramatic swill will you self-absorbed intellectuals conjure up next?

I don't blame you for not visiting. I'm afraid I'm not very good company. But, lo, something is afoot. I'll let you know soon.

Your brother,
Ray

Chapter 8

Blake Stallone stood next to the kitchen sink and poured a second cup of Maxwell House into his NYPD coffee mug. He watched the steam rise from the scalding beverage and coalesce on the kitchen window like fingers of a ghostly hand. Hearing the crunch of gravel, he leaned forward and squinted out the window, scanning the driveway. "I'll be damned," he muttered to himself. Alice Thornberry was pulling up to the trailer in her rusted-out Jeep Cherokee. Blake looked at his watch: 7:00 a.m. "I'll be damned." He walked out of the kitchen and made his way to the trailer door. Pushing the door open and leaning out, he encountered a flock of red and orange leaves whirling in the wind before him, as if funneled by some invisible hand to play havoc with both innocent and guilty bystanders.

Alice slowly climbed out of the Jeep, her old bones grinding with belabored strife. "Mornin', Blake," Alice hollered as she pattered up to the trailer in a long, bulky, hooded parka that hung down to the tops of her untied, dilapidated hiking boots.

"Hi, Alice. What brings you out this blustery mornin'?"

Alice peered out from beneath the hood of her parka. From where Blake stood, she appeared to be a lost child peeking out from some dark, underground province into a well-lit but unsettled world.

"Blake, I could be in a bit of trouble."

Blake furrowed his brow and winced. "You ain't kiddin', are you?"

"No. I ain't."

Blake nodded and jutted out his jaw. "Well. Come on in, then."

Chapter 9

Rick Applegate exhaled a heavy sigh and slowly swiveled in his desk chair, the worn metal hardware squeaking adamantly. "Well, I understand. It's just that she's an old woman and a friend of mine at that." Rick held the phone receiver away from his ear. The FBI agent on the other end of the line talked so loud it was making Rick's head ache. "Well, I know that. Sure. Sure. Okay. Thanks for your input." Rick hung up the phone and rubbed his offended ear.

Walt Dropo stared at the nameplate on his boss's desk. *Richard Applegate. Sheriff of Halfmoon.* "So what'd he say?"

Gently rubbing his tired eyes, the sheriff could smell the residue of tobacco on his brown-stained fingertips. "He said we've got to look at Alice. We've got to look at her real hard."

Walt Dropo shook his head as he walked over to his desk and sat on the front edge. "Why did you call the FBI in the first place?"

"That's the procedure. They like to keep track of the odd-ball stuff out here in the hinterland." Rick shrugged. "Just doing my job."

Walt shook his head and smirked judgmentally. "Well, I wouldn't want to be in your shoes when you break the news to Alice. She's gonna be real pissed off."

Rick got up from his chair and hitched up his green khaki pants. He smiled malevolently. "If you don't quit whining, I'll send you out to question her."

Walt felt a hot spray of adrenaline cascading through his legs. "Uh, you wouldn't do that to me, would you?"

Rick shook his head dismissively. "We'll see."

Chapter 10

Alice Thornberry sipped her hot Maxwell House coffee. It burned her bottom lip and the tip of her tongue. Staring down at the scratched surface of the wooden kitchen table, she paid the discomfort no mind.

Blake Stallone considered her for several moments. He reckoned she needed both space and time on her side. Finally, he spoke. "Talk to me, Alice."

Alice continued to stare down at the table. "I've come to you because I know you were in homicide. In New York."

"Yes, that's true."

"I need some good advice from someone who knows about these things."

"What things?"

Alice swallowed hard. "Killin' things."

Blake took a deep breath and leaned back in his straight-backed, wooden chair. "I don't follow you, Alice. Can you spell it out for me?"

Alice's eyes traced a purposeful arc as she surveyed the inner depths of her ravaged mind. "It's a long story. You sure you got time to listen to me?"

"Sure, Alice. I got time. Why don't you just start at the beginnin'."

Alice raised her head and looked Blake squarely in the eyes. "We've been friends a long time. Knowed each other since we was kids. I think you know me pretty well. Wouldn't you say so?"

"Yeah. I'd say that's true."

"And you knew Jed. You knew him pretty well too."

"Yep. That's true."

"And you know I loved him. As crazy as he could get, I always loved him."

Blake nodded in agreement.

Alice blinked her eyes rapidly. Fighting back the tears, she whispered, "I killed Jed. Like he was some animal by the side of the road. I killed him dead."

Blake felt his heart quicken in disquietude. "Now hold on, Alice. Jed's been missin' for ten years. Nobody even knows what happened to him. He just disappeared."

Alice returned her stare to the surface of the wooden table. "I know what happened. I've always knowed."

Blake rolled his eyes with some small measure of exasperation. He had a feeling where this was going, and the feeling wasn't good. He held his cup of hot coffee in both hands. The warmth inched its way pleasantly into his arthritic wrists. "Alice, can you do somethin' for me? Can you start way back at the beginnin'? Can you take me through this nice and slow?"

Alice sipped her coffee. She didn't taste a thing. "Yeah. I can do that."

Chapter 11

Aaron Riley stoked the logs in his wood-burning potbelly stove with peaceful circumspection. The warmth radiating from the iron heater made the hair on his arms curl. He smiled. Winter was coming. And he was ready. He had chopped and stacked three cords of seasoned firewood. Some hickory. Some elm. Yeah, he was ready.

Aaron had been up since 5:00 a.m., reading the one book he possessed. He got up every morning at five and read the same book. Read it carefully, for about two hours, digesting every word and nuance of meaning. And once he finished the book, he'd start over again at the beginning. That was the way they had told him to read it. They'd told him it was the only book he'd ever need. And Aaron did what they said.

Chapter 12

"Can I ask a favor of you, Blake?"

"Sure, Alice."

Alice Thornberry pushed her cup of coffee to the side. She needed something stronger. Something more suitable for the conversation at hand. "Can you get me a taste of bourbon?"

Blake Stallone cocked his head to the side. "Bourbon? Alice, it's seven in the morning."

"I know what time it is!" Alice retorted nastily. Then she composed herself. "It's just that it's gonna be hard for me to tell you what I'm gonna tell you."

Blake shrugged his shoulders and relented. He got up from his chair and walked over to the tall, narrow pantry next to the refrigerator. *What can she tell me that I haven't seen or heard before?* he thought as he pulled a bottle off the top shelf. He returned to the kitchen table and placed the bottle in front of Alice. "You finished with your coffee?"

"Yeah. I'm finished."

Blake grabbed her mug and rinsed it out at the sink. Then he brought the mug back to Alice and placed it on the table in front of her.

Alice stared at the bottle of bourbon. Old Grand-dad. She uncorked the vessel and poured a couple of ounces of the golden brown libation into her chalice. Savoring a medicinal sip and smacking her lips, the old woman sat quietly for a few moments, allowing the magical tonic to splash into her bloodstream. "Now. That's better." She picked at the corner of her mouth with arthritic fingers. "Blake, what nobody knows is that Jed was sick. He wasn't right in a lot of ways. He had a bad liver from all the drinkin', so he couldn't drink no more. He had arthritis so bad he couldn't shoot his rifle no more, and he couldn't fish. But the worst of it was his memory. Half the time he was so confused, he didn't want to get outta bed. Christ, some days he'd wake up and look at me like I was some fuckin' Martian. Really. He didn't know who the hell I was."

Blake sipped his coffee. He contemplated the steam rising from the mug, ghostly fragments of evaporating water molecules. "He had dementia, Alice. That's why he couldn't remember you."

"Well, I don't know what the hell it was. But it was damn sad."

Blake nodded his head, motioning for Alice to continue.

"Well, what happened was this. One day, Jed says to me, 'Alice, I want you to shoot me. I don't want to live no more. Can't do anything I like, so what's the point in livin'? I want you to shoot me.'" Alice shook her head and stared down at the table. "I said to him, 'Jed, if you want to be shot, go ahead and shoot yourself. I'm not gonna do it.' And then Jed said, 'For Christ's sake, Alice, I've already tried. Down in the sugarhouse. I tried, but couldn't do it. I tried riggin' up the shotgun with some string and a pulley system. But it didn't work. Fuckin' gun slipped to the side and blew a hole through the wall of the sugarhouse.'" Alice shook her head and looked up at Blake. Tears were caught in the wrinkles of her old, worn face. "Jed just wanted to die. That's all he wanted."

Blake scratched at the beard stubble on his chin. "Go on, Alice. Tell me the whole story."

Alice belted back another hit of Old Grand-dad. She felt warm and secure. Bourbon did that for her. "Well, I thought about it. About killin' him. And I thought, you know, I might be able to do it with a shovel. I knew I couldn't shoot him. No, sir. But maybe I could hit him with a shovel." Alice scratched her pointy chin with cracked fingernails that were some shade of yellow. "So I told Jed about the shovel idea. You know what he did when I told him? You know what he did? He cried. He cried because I had made him so happy." Alice considered what she had just said. "I don't think I'd ever seen him happier than when I told him I was gonna kill him." Alice shook her head, grunted, and tossed back the rest of her bourbon.

Blake took a deep breath and got up out of his chair. He grabbed his coffee mug, carried it to the sink, and washed it out. Returning to the table with mug in hand, the retired detective sat down and checked his watch. "Alice, you're drivin' me to drink at seven fifteen in the mornin'." Blake grabbed the bottle of Old Grand-dad and half-filled the earthenware vessel. As if searching for the answers to life's penetrating questions, he studied the 80-proof firewater before tossing it back and wincing while the burn of the golden fluid made its deliberate way down. "All right, Alice. I think I'm ready to hear the grand finale."

Alice nodded and pursed her lips. "Well, this is what we did. We said we'd wait till April so the ground would be nice and soft. Then one mornin'—I remember it was April 9th—Jed came into the kitchen, poured a cup of coffee, and drank it down. Then he said to me, 'Let's go do it. Let's do it now.' I didn't want to know what he meant. But I did." Alice shrugged her skinny shoulders. "Life is fuckin' strange, ain't it?"

"Yeah. It is."

"Well, me and Jed filled a flask with I.W. Harper, threw a shovel in the back of the truck, and headed south on Snake Hollow Road. We turned in on the utility drive like we was goin' to the sugarhouse. We drove up the drive a ways and then swung the truck into the woods and parked it. We took the shovel and walked south into the woods until we crossed over onto the Slaughter property." Alice paused in reflection and shook her head. "Emma Slaughter told me once that she'd never sell that property. She wanted to just let it be." Alice smirked. "You can't depend on nothin' in this life."

Blake nodded. *That's for goddamned sure*, he thought.

"Well, we found a good spot in a clearin' where the ground was thawed and soft. We shared in the diggin' of the grave. Jed would dig and I would sit. And then I would dig and Jed would sit. I remember sittin' there on a big ol' log, drinkin' my bourbon, surprised at how blank my mind was. I was about to kill my husband, and my mind was just dead. I guess that happens when you're about to do somethin' crazy."

Blake sipped the Old Grand-dad. "I expect so."

Alice stared into her coffee mug. Stared at the bourbon coating the bottom of the vessel. "I wonder what Jed was thinkin' when he was sittin' there and I was diggin'? I wonder if his mind was blank too?"

Blake nodded. "I expect it probably was."

Alice shook her head and pinched her crusty lips with the fingers of her right hand. "Anyway, once we dug the grave, it was time to do it. Jed climbed down into the hole. I handed him the flask, and he took a good pull off it. Then he handed it back to me, and I laid it on the ground. I remember thinkin' how much I would need a drink after I did what had to be done." Alice wiped her mouth with the back of her hand. Her jaws clenched spasmodically. "I picked up the shovel and looked at Jed down there in the hole. He looked so small down there. Like a little boy. It was like I didn't even know him anymore. Like maybe I never knew him at all." Alice scratched at the back of her head. "Jed stared up at me. He said, 'Don't fuckin' miss.'" Alice sat quietly for a moment. "'Don't fuckin' miss.' Those were the last words he said to me." Alice poured another substantial slosh of bourbon into her coffee mug. Staring into it, she saw unforgiving traces of deeds done long ago. "Then he turned his back to me. And I hit him. Hit him square on the back of the head." Alice nodded demonstratively. "I didn't miss."

Blake cautiously leaned back in his chair. His gut was burning from the mixture of bourbon and coffee churning away at a dormant ulcer. "Then what happened?"

Alice sipped the Old Grand-dad. Her stomach felt just fine. "I drank down what was left in the flask, and then I filled the hole up with dirt. Then I took the shovel and walked back to the truck."

"Did you get rid of the shovel?"

"Me and Jed talked about that. I did what he told me to do."

"And what was that?"

"I threw it in the Ottaquechee River."

"Where in the river?"

"I threw it off the bridge at the Quechee Gorge."

Blake raised his eyebrows. "Hmmm."

Alice looked at him quizzically. "What do you mean, 'hmmm'?"

Blake smiled sheepishly. "I meant that was smart of you. That shovel will never be found."

Alice rubbed her wrinkled forehead with the palm of her right hand. Her left was wrapped securely around her coffee mug. "Well, I'm glad you think so."

Blake scratched the back of his sun-baked neck, eyes squinting with some inner reckoning. "What'd you do with the truck?"

"Me and Jed talked about that too. I drove the truck back to the service drive and dumped the shovel down in some sticker bushes. Then I took the truck down to the sugarhouse and left it there with the keys in the ignition."

Blake nodded. "Go on."

"Then I walked home."

"You left the shovel in the sticker bushes?"

"Yep, I did. After the truck was found, and Sheriff Rick gave it back to me, that's when I got rid of the shovel."

Blake stared at Alice, configuring in his mind the movements of her felony. "What are you gonna do now, Alice?"

Alice looked at Blake. Looked at him as if he were the village idiot. "I ain't gonna do nothin'." Alice swallowed the last of her bourbon. "You ain't gonna say anything, are you?"

"No."

Alice nodded her head. "Well, okay then."

Chapter 13

Aaron Riley heard a dull thud conveyed through the windowpane. Putting down his coffee, he got up from the dining room table, hitched up his jeans, and lumbered over to the window. He looked out into the stark and windswept desolation of the ashen morning. Nothing but leaves whirling about in the small clearing in the forest. He leaned on the window sill and looked down. There it was. An evening grosbeak. Lying on its back. Tiny, brittle legs moving spasmodically. Its brown head bobbing up and down, its conical bill mouthing a silent song of distress.

Aaron dashed out the front door and onto the porch. He leaped down the short stairway and quickly moved around to the side of the cabin. The grosbeak lay still in a clump of leaves, an unexpected gift dropped from the heavens, its bright yellow chest shining in the morning gray like some unforecasted light.

Leaning down carefully on one knee, Aaron gently cradled the bird in the palm of his left hand. He carried the ailing avian into the house, grabbing a white linen napkin from the dining room table on his way to the kitchen. He placed the napkin in a wooden breadbasket sitting on the kitchen table and carefully laid the large finch on the napkin. The bird lay there. Quiet. Aaron stared at the still creature. He caressed the black, brown, and white tail feathers with his bulky fingers. The bird's stillness had the look of permanence. Eyes wide open. Eyes like glass. Like mysterious, delicate crystals from a shaman's bag of white-magic amulets.

Lifting and cradling the bird in the palms of his hands, Aaron regarded it reverently as a sacred icon, evidence of something good here on earth, and drew it to his mouth. He took a deep breath, pursed his lips, and gently blew on the motionless creature from head to tail. Over its head, he softly chanted a sacred mantram. OM HREEM. OM HREEM. OM HREEM. He inhaled deeply once again, pursed his lips, and blew on the bird from head to tail. He considered the dear creature. A creature of God. The avian eyes began to move in their dried-out sockets. Aaron could sense the life force regenerate in the creature's body as it stared at him from some faraway shore. It turned its head to the left. And then to the right. As if to confirm that its head was still connected to its body.

Aaron gently returned the bird to the breadbasket.

Chapter 14

October 22, 2000

Dear Ray,

I am so pleased by your letter. You seem to be infinitely better. Whatever they're doing for you at Sheppard Pratt seems to be working. And what exactly is afoot? I'm intrigued.

Guess who called me last night? Jane Humphrey. She ran into Harvey, and he mentioned to her that I was on sabbatical and writing a book on ethics. Well, you know Jane. She wanted to know all the ins and outs of my plans for the book. Of course, I had to make something up on the fly. Hell, I haven't given a minute's thought to the damn thing. At any rate, in an attempt to be helpful, she articulated a long dissertation on the theory that the history of Western intellectual life has been nothing other than a 2500-year battle between the ideologies of Apollo and Dionysius. True to form, Jane asserted that the underbelly of the life force cannot and will not be denied. That in the end, Apollo triumphs only when it is in nature's interest to do so. Yes, sir, Raymond, Jane ain't no campus pinhead.

Last night, I was drinking wine (I've been doing a lot of that lately) and reading a bit of Samuel Johnson. I came across an interesting quote, referred to by Johnson, from Shakespeare's **Measure for Measure:**

Thou hast nor youth, nor age,
But as it were an after-dinner's sleep,
Dreaming on both.

Well, little brother, if this life is really but a dream, I'd like to meet the special-effects director! 'Cause it sure seems real to me!

Well, my brain is beginning to get jumpy (too much vino, I dare say). So I'll close for now. I want you to know that I feel bad about not visiting you. The last time was just too distressing for me. You were in pretty bad shape. So for the time being, let's agree to keep writing.

I miss you.
Alexander

Chapter 15

Madeline Kerr walked to the end of the bar, pushed open the swinging door leading to the kitchen, and leaned in. "Susan, can you get Roy to watch the bar for ten minutes? I've got something to take care of."

Susan looked up from the stove. Her auburn hair was pulled back into a black hairnet, and her crooked smile revealed the need for dental care. "Yeah. I'll get him. He's out back."

"Thanks."

Madeline walked out into the barroom. She navigated her way through the crowd to the back end where Alexander Lessing was playing pool with a couple of locals. She motioned to Alex that she wanted to see him.

Alex excused himself and walked over to Madeline. "Hey, Maddy. What can I do for you?"

"Is there any way I can pull you out of the game? Just for ten minutes?"

"Sure. No problem." Alex turned to his friends. "I'm going to talk with Maddy for a few minutes. I'll be back."

Jim Robertson looked up from the pool table and cast an ornery glare at Alex. Jim was obese and sported a bushy, white beard. He looked like Santa Claus. "Don't get yourself into any trouble, now."

Alex laughed. "You mean female trouble?"

Jim playfully massaged the pool cue with both hands. "That's the worst kind."

Alex turned to Madeline. "What's up?"

Madeline tilted her head toward an empty booth. "Let's sit over there."

The two good souls walked to the booth and sat down opposite one another. Madeline pensively rubbed her hands together. "I want to ask you something. I think you might be able to help me."

Alex smiled and nodded his head. He liked being consulted. It made him feel powerful. And he liked feeling powerful. Especially around women. "Sure. Go ahead."

"Well, I'm interested in becoming more spiritual."

Alex smiled and shook his head. "Spiritual? What do you mean by 'spiritual'?"

Madeline smiled impishly. "It sounds stupid, but I found a book lying in the parking lot behind the bar. I asked everyone who works here if they had lost it, but no one claimed it. Anyway, I read the book and it inspired me."

"What's the name of the book?"

"Zen Mind, Beginner's Mind. It was written by Shunryu Suzuki."

Alex nodded knowingly. "Shunryu Suzuki. He established the first Zen Center in America."

"Have you read the book?"

"Yes. Several times. I too was impressed."

Madeline wrinkled her cute nose like a child who's feeling bewitched. "The book made sense to me. I really want to pursue this Zen way of life."

Alex's eyes twinkled. Madeline was in luck. She didn't know it yet, but she was. "Maddy, have you ever heard of Thich Nhat Hanh?"

"No."

"Thich Nhat Hanh is a Vietnamese Zen Buddhist. He is a very gifted teacher."

Madeline nodded intently. She wanted to know more.

"Thich Nhat Hanh has established two spiritual communities in the United States. One is in California." Alex cocked his head playfully. "Do you know where the other one is located?"

Madeline smiled and shrugged her shoulders. "I'm afraid I don't."

"Well, I think you're a very lucky woman."

"I am?"

"Yes. You are."

Madeline leaned against the backrest of the booth. She knew Alex was toying with her. "Okay. Why am I so lucky?"

"You know the Skunk Hollow Tavern? Over at Hartland-Four Corners?"

"Sure. I've been there a hundred times."

"Well, if you're on Route 12 and you go just past the Skunk, there's a dirt road. If you take that road about a half-mile back, you'll find the Green Mountain Dharma Center. That's Thich Nhat Hanh's place."

Madeline wrinkled her brow. She was anticipatory and confused at the same time. "Really? There's a spiritual community back behind the Skunk?"

"There sure is. If you want to know what Zen Buddhism is about, that's the place to learn."

Madeline felt her chest grow heavy and then light, as if some momentous cloud of indecision weighed on her momentarily and then disappeared. "I'll be damned. Isn't that something?"

Alex held Maddy in his gaze and pondered her raw beauty. He had always found her attractive. But now there was something magnetic about her. Beneath the surface of her respectful attitude, he sensed some wild energy that longed for expression. Alex got up from the booth. He stood over Maddy and crossed his arms. "So what are you going to do?"

Maddy nodded. "Well, I think I'm going over to Hartland. Check this place out."

"Good. Keep me posted on your journey."

Maddy smirked. "I wouldn't call going to Hartland a journey. It's less than a half-hour away."

Alex shook his head. She just didn't get it. "The path to a deep understanding of Zen will be a journey. It will be filled with dangerous curves and precipitous cliffs." The moment the words came out of his mouth, he felt stupid. As if he really knew anything about spiritual journeys. And yet, that was the way he was. He acted as if he had personally experienced the content of all the ideas he had contemplated in his vast reading of the world's philosophical landscape. Nothing could be further from the truth.

Maddy shrugged her shoulders. She felt inadequate. For a moment, she was sorry she had shared this secret dream of spirituality with someone she believed was a friend. But then common sense prevailed. "Okay. I'll let you know how it goes."

Alex walked back to his pool game. Jim Robertson handed Alex his pool cue and winked at him. "You gonna get some of that?"

Alex shook his head. He was disheartened. The thing was, he *did* want some of that. But at the same time, he respected Maddy's longing for spiritual fulfillment. And he didn't like

Jim Robertson's joking about it. "Don't think so, Jim," said Alex.

"Well, what the hell did she want?"

"Jim, some things are personal. Let's just leave it at that."

Jim took a long draw off his Budweiser. "I swear to God! You go talk to a woman for five minutes, and all the fun is sucked right out of you." He shook his head in disgust.

Chapter 16

Walt Dropo dragged his tired, lanky body out of the Halfmoon Police squad car, stood up and therapeutically maneuvered his stiff back, and slammed the door. He was none too happy about what he'd been ordered to do. He could still see Rick Applegate's smirking, malevolent face.

Walt hitched up his khaki pants and headed for the front door of Alice Thornberry's clapboard farmhouse. The house was nearly a hundred years old and had seen better days. Walt thumped up the porch steps and stopped in front of the door. It was closed, and he stood there for a few moments, reckoning how he would say what he had to say. He turned his back to the door and stared out at the tall white poplars swaying in the breeze, dancing to some internal song of nature. Walt shrugged his shoulders. He hated confrontation. *Ah, fuck it!*

Walt turned back to the front door. *"Shit, Alice!"* Walt stumbled back a few paces. He felt his heart banging wildly behind his sternum. "Christ, Alice, you scared the hell out of me."

The doorway framed a poised Alice Thornberry garbed in a dark green flannel shirt and a pair of blue overalls. Her wiry, gray hair stood out from her skull as if electrified. She smiled sardonically. "This mornin' I oiled the hinges on the front door. Opens mighty quiet, don't it?"

Walt had caught his breath and was trying to regain whatever semblance of composure he may have had. "Yeah. I'd say you did a good job. Use the WD-40?"

"Yeah."

"Okay. Good."

Alice leaned against the doorjamb and let Walt sweat a little. She didn't want to be of any help whatsoever to the Halfmoon Police. No, sir.

Walt shifted his weight nervously. His feet felt as if they were glued to the porch.

Alice smiled wryly. "Rick called me about five minutes ago. Told me you were comin'."

Walt nodded his head. He was downright embarrassed. "Yeah. Well, I gotta ask you some questions. About Jed. Is that okay?"

"Don't look like I got much of a choice."

Walt shrugged. "Yeah. That's about right, I guess."

Alice backed out of the doorway and into the house. Walt stood where he was, looking in. He could smell a dank mustiness coming from inside.

"Well, get your ass in here!" yelled Alice.

Walt hitched up his pants and walked in. Closing the door behind him, he could hear Alice rummaging in the kitchen. He walked through the dark, cluttered living room and the dark, cluttered dining room. Alice had no use for lights in the daytime. All they did was jack up the electric bill.

Alice was warming a pot of corn chowder on the stove. The aroma was sweet, like spring sassafras permeating a sunny meadow. Alice bent over the pot with a long, wooden spoon and took a sip. She nodded her head, certifying its tastiness. "You want some soup, Walt?"

Walt sat down at the Formica-topped kitchen table. He stared at the faded pink and white paisley designs that seemed to be floating on the table's surface. "No. I'm not hungry."

Alice claimed a clean bowl from the cupboard above the sink and ladled some soup into it. Then she picked up a dirty spoon from the countertop, rinsed it off, and brought her meal to the table. She sat down across from Walt and started eating the soup. She slurped up the chowder as if in some strange state of isolation. As if Walt weren't even there. Finally, she put her spoon down and looked up. "So you gonna ask me questions or not?"

Walt pulled a notepad and ballpoint pen out of the breast pocket of his blue oxford shirt. He swallowed hard. "Alice, I don't like this any more than you do. It ain't personal. It's just business."

Alice shook her head and smirked. "Let's just get it over with."

Walt nodded and inhaled deeply. He could feel a deep burn eddying in the pit of his stomach. "Alice, I need you to account for your whereabouts on the day Jed disappeared. Can you do that for me?"

Alice smiled halfheartedly. "Walt, that was *ten* years ago. I can hardly remember what I did last week, much less ten years ago."

Walt cocked his head to the side, not without sympathy. "Just do the best you can. All right?"

Alice nodded her head. Her shoulders slumped as if in a state of surrender. "All I remember was Jed gettin' up in the mornin', havin' his cup of coffee, and then drivin' off in his truck. Said he was goin' down to the sugarhouse."

"About what time was that, Alice?"

"Oh, hell, I don't know. Maybe eight or nine."

"And you never saw him again?"

"Never saw him again."

"And what did *you* do that day?"

Alice rolled her eyes. "Walt, let me ask *you* a question. What the hell did *you* do on the day Jed disappeared? Huh? You go ahead and tell me."

Walt let out a long sigh. The burn in his stomach was spiraling up into his esophagus. "I don't know, Alice." Walt blinked his eyes hard. "So you're tellin' me you don't remember?"

Alice gnawed on her bottom lip with what was left of her top row of teeth. "That's what I'm tellin' you."

"Do you remember if Jed had any enemies? Anybody who might want to hurt him?"

"Walt, you're beginnin' to piss me off. Why don't you go back to Jed's case file and see what I said back when Jed went missin'. Wouldn't that make a lot more sense than comin' out here ten years later and botherin' the hell out of me?"

Walt dropped his head and sulked. He stared at the paisley fish swimming around on the tabletop. "There ain't no file to look at. We lost the goddamn thing."

Alice flashed a mischievous smile that Walt didn't see. "Well, that ain't my problem."

Walt took an exasperated breath and looked up from the table. "No, I reckon it ain't."

Alice spooned out the remainder of her chowder and ate it. She got up from the table, walked to the sink, and placed the bowl and spoon into it. She stared at weary Walt sulking at the table. She almost felt sorry for him. "What I want to know, Walt, is why you're askin' me all these questions. You think I killed Jed? Is that what you think?"

Walt looked up. His eyes were tired and bloodshot. "Hell, no, Alice. I don't think you killed Jed. It's just that in cases like this, we gotta look at the spouse real hard. That's the way police business works. You always look at the spouse first."

Alice squinted her eyes and smirked. "Well, after you look at the spouse, then what? Who do you look at then?"

Walt got up from the table and scratched aimlessly at the back of his neck. He shook his head. "I don't know. I really don't know." He stared down at his brown leather shoes atop the maple-planked kitchen floor. His shoes seemed a long way away. "Alice, I gotta ask you one more question. Would you take me out to the shed? Would you let me look at the tools you got out there?"

Alice stared at Walt, who continued to stare at his shoes. "Damn. You're a real asshole. You know that?"

Walt clenched his teeth, his gaze fixated floorward. "Please, Alice. Then I'll leave."

Alice shook her head dismissively. "The shed's open. Do whatever you want out there."

Walt slowly raised his head and stared at Alice. He said not a word. But his eyes spoke to her. They said he was sorry. He turned and walked out the kitchen door.

Alice stood at the sink and watched him through the kitchen window as he walked to the toolshed. A half-smile appeared spontaneously around her mouth, and she felt the corners of her dried lips curl upward. *Look at the spouse. You got that right.*

Chapter 17

Madeline Kerr stopped her baby blue Ford Rancher pickup at the traffic light in Hartland-Four Corners. The midafternoon air was cold and crisp, and the sky was clear except for a scattering of wispy, ivory clouds scrawled across the heavens like abstract signatures written by the hands of indifferent giants. She turned right at the light, drove past the Skunk Hollow Tavern, and made the first right onto Town Farm Hill Road. The uphill dirt road was pretty much washed out, and as it banked steeply, it seemed to Madeline that if she were to take it to its end, she might become airborne.

Madeline navigated the ruts in the road as if she were a gymnast performing a challenging maneuver on the parallel beams. About a half-mile up, she made a hard left onto Ayers Lane. Immediately, she was under a canopy of evergreens. Eying the shadowed, narrow lane as it vanished into the horizon, she felt as if she were in some metaphysical time tunnel where life and death might very well merge seamlessly.

She traversed the tree-lined tunnel and was suddenly rushed by a grand, open sky resting effortlessly on undulating hills of golden grasses. Dotting the open landscape were a few modest, gray clapboard houses and a red barn. In the distance straight ahead, she could see a two-story house that somehow called her to attention. On her immediate right was a field where visitors had pulled in their vehicles and parked. Madeline checked out the license plates. Montana. Vermont. New York. Connecticut. Maryland. Madeline pulled her truck into the field and parked next to an old, rusted-out Buick. She turned off the engine and stared out across the landscape of lustrous reeds. A lazy wind gently moved the crested tips of the yellow stalks, creating a ballet of gesturing waves directed from the earthly realm to the infinite sky above. She felt her heart beating rapidly and knew she was at one of life's unavoidable crossroads.

Collecting her thoughts, Maddy hopped out of the truck, stretched her legs a bit, and began walking toward the road. When she lifted her gaze, she stopped dead in her tracks. The glowing sun, set like some jewel of antiquity on the crest of the rolling, green mountains in the near distance, mesmerized her. Her ears buzzed pleasantly within a vast silence that seemed to create an insulated vacuum in which the Green Mountain Dharma Center mysteriously floated. She breathed the rarefied mountain air deep into her lungs and knew she was in the presence of the holy.

Meandering up the road toward the gray house in the distance, she was all the while mindful of the quiet and calm resonating from the country abode. When she arrived at the house, she was uncertain about which door to address, the front or the side. She opted for the side door and went in, finding herself in a small, stone-floored foyer occupied by nothing but benches and open, doorless closets. A few pairs of hiking boots were lined up neatly under the benches, and some winter coats and hats hung in the closets. Madeline smiled quizzically and sat down on one of the benches. She removed her hiking boots, slipped them under the bench, and then removed her coat and hung it up in one of the closets. She liked the simplicity of acting in the present moment with few choices. But then another decision presented itself. Two closed doors faced each other across the foyer. The sign declared the door on the right for *Staff*, while the sign on the opposite door indicated the *Kitchen*. Which door to approach? She selected the kitchen. Knocking gently and slowly opening the door, she leaned in and saw two young Asian women with shaved heads tending a large pot of soup. Each woman wore a green apron over a maroon turtleneck sweater and long, black skirt.

"Excuse me," Madeline said. "I'm looking for someone who could introduce me to the Dharma Center. It's my first visit here."

The two young women smiled and nodded and then returned to their ministrations over the soup pot. Not exactly knowing what to do, Madeline entered the kitchen and closed the door behind her. To her immediate right, she saw a small dining area with a modest library. A tall, thin, Caucasian woman of uncertain age was setting a table for dinner. She too wore the turtleneck sweater and long skirt. Madeline approached her. "Excuse me. I was wondering if you could arrange for someone to talk to me about the Dharma Center. It's my first visit here."

The woman looked up and smiled gently. "One moment," she said and returned to setting the last place. When she finished, she approached Madeline and stood in front of her. She held her hands together loosely, palm in palm, in front of her heart. "How can I help you?"

Madeline felt uncomfortably odd about having to make her request a third time in the last ninety seconds. "I was hoping someone here would be able to tell me about the Dharma Center. Perhaps give me a guided tour?"

The woman smiled and gently bowed her head. "There really is no tour to give. You are free to walk the grounds and go wherever you like."

Madeline nodded and waited hopefully for the woman to continue. She was met with still silence. "Perhaps you could tell me something about Thich Nhat Hanh? I'm planning on reading some of his books."

The woman motioned to the tiny library in the corner of the room. "Feel free to read any of Thay's books. And feel free to meditate with the monks here at the Dharma Center." The woman stared at Madeline with creamy, gray eyes that seemed to be peering out at her from some distant shore.

"Well, thank you. Perhaps I'll do that."

The woman smiled sweetly. Then, seemingly out of nowhere, a deep, melodious gong sounded. The woman bowed her head and closed her eyes. Her breathing was very steady, very centered. She remained in this repose for about thirty seconds. Then she spoke. "At the sound of the gong, we stop whatever we're doing and return to the present moment. It is in the present moment that we touch the peace within ourselves."

Madeline nodded, not knowing what else to do.

The woman opened her eyes wide. "When you're taking your walk, stop at the red barn. That's the meditation hall."

"Oh, okay. I will."

The woman smiled mysteriously and walked into the kitchen. She donned an apron and began chopping vegetables for the salad.

Madeline stood still for a few moments, considering what had just transpired. She wrinkled her freckled nose. *No bullshit here. Say what you mean and get on with life.* She smiled and walked back to the foyer.

Chapter 18

The red barn lay in a shallow valley about a quarter of a mile down the road. The sun was starting its downward turn, the temperature was dropping fast, and the once-clear sky was now populated by heavy, gray clouds signifying that snow was ahead. Madeline Kerr pulled the collar of her winter coat snuggly around the back of her neck. When the cold comes in Vermont, it imposes itself severely like a heavy burden from which relief is denied.

When she arrived at the barn, she turned and looked from whence she had come. In the distance, she saw a solitary woman walking up the road toward the gray house. Bundled up in a long, black coat, the figure plodded along as if she were in some kind of meditative trance. Madeline reflected on the woman. Reflected on the lone, black form on the horizon. The lone, black form under gray cloud cover, surrounded by golden grasses undulating in the breeze and waving to the heavens. Madeline wondered if anyone or anything populated the heavens. Was anyone or anything looking down at the strange and inscrutable earthbound drama? Madeline gathered herself and wondered where in the world these thoughts of hers came from. It was as if they were transmitted to her from beyond. As if the thoughts were not originating within her, but rather being received by her from some transcendent source. She shrugged and turned back to the barn.

Walking through the entrance, the receptive seeker found herself in a narrow, horizontal foyer, with glass windows behind her looking out on the Dharma Center grounds, and glass windows before her looking into the meditation hall. Benches ran along the sides of the foyer, on her left and right, and above the benches, coat hooks protruded from the walls. She looked down and saw a single pair of hiking boots under one of the benches. She peered through a window into the meditation hall. The hall, constructed entirely of knotty pine, was in the shape of a dome, and had thick, gray, wall-to-wall carpeting. At the far end of the hall was an eight-foot-tall, soft-pink-colored stone Buddha sitting in the lotus posture. The face of the Buddha exhibited a smile reflecting both peacefulness and acceptance. Madeline liked the simplicity of the hall. Nothing ostentatious. Nothing unnecessary. She leaned close to the glass window, looking from side to side, in search of the lone meditator. *Ah, there he is.* Off in the front right quadrant of the hall, lying flat on his back, was a prodigious hulk of a man, deep in meditation. Madeline stared at the man, blinked a few times, and resumed staring. *I'll be damned,* she thought.

Chapter 19

Rick Applegate leaned back in his chair, feet up on his desk. He pulled a long draw off his Arturo Fuente robusto cigar and blew a thin stream of blue smoke up to the ceiling. "So tell me about it, Walt."

Walt Dropo stood in front of the sheriff's desk, anxiously jingling some change in his right pocket. "I'm still pissed at you for sendin' me up there. It just ain't right."

Rick shook his head dismissively. "Get over it." He stared at his inept deputy. "And stop fooling around with that goddamn change."

Walt removed his hand from his pocket and reflexively bowed his head as if he were an abused child. "Well, I talked to her just like you wanted."

"And?"

"Well, she doesn't remember much about the day Jed went missin' except for him comin' down for coffee and then drivin' to the sugarhouse in his truck." Walt kicked the dingy linoleum floor with the toe of his boot. "And then she said I should look in Jed's file if I wanted answers to questions from ten years ago, and I told her there wasn't no file. Not anymore."

Rick smiled and rolled his eyes. He could hardly see Walt through the thick curtain of smoke produced by his fine, fat cigar. "What about the toolshed? What did you find there?"

"Nothin'."

"No shovels or anything?"

"A couple snow shovels from True Value. Still had the sales stickers on 'em from 1996."

"Hmmm. Nineteen ninety-six doesn't do us much good."

"Nope." Walt put his right hand back in his pocket and started jingling the change again.

Rick sighed deeply and looked up at the gray paint peeling off the ceiling. The nicotine from the cigar was making his toes throb. "All right, Walt. Go on home."

Walt looked at his watch: 5:15 p.m. He nodded at Rick, threw on his coat, and walked out the door.

Rick Applegate drew on his cigar and directed a final plume of smoke toward the ceiling. He was fifty-six years old. He was tired. Tired of his job. Tired of his wife. Tired of Walt Dropo. He considered himself for a moment and decided that he was tired of himself. *I just might have to do something about that,* he thought.

Chapter 20

He stood in the evening darkness, on frozen dirt and strands of brown, frost-hardened grass, in the dense, black thicket of leafless sticker bushes. He saw his murky, white breath hovering before him like a ghostly veil on the dispersed yellow light coming from inside the trailer. Snow was beginning to fall, the flakes dotting his black T-shirt like aberrant lodestars. He paid no mind to the cold. He felt the flakes lighting upon his bare face and right arm like friendly ladybugs that had forgotten their season had passed. At one point, he would have felt the flakes like phantoms on his left arm. But no more. That arm was long gone. Ten years gone. The left sleeve of his black T-shirt just hung there, loose, like a bad dream that wouldn't end.

He looked down and raised his left foot and placed his boot on the sturdy hand guard of the Husqvarna 575XP chainsaw. He stared at the trailer through black, godless eyes. Glass eyes, behind which there was no conscience, no soul.

Chapter 21

A whirlwind of surging oppositional forces engulf him in a sea of desiring strife such that no degree of equanimity can be calibrated from points north, south, east, or west. But then he turns inward. And sees an open door. And goes through the door to a timeless and spaceless milieu. A milieu of equanimity. Equanimity so permanent that it appears solid. A solidity with omnipresent eyes that witness with calm perspicacity the sea of desiring strife and all that it encompasses.

Aaron Riley sat straight up in bed. Turned on the bedside lamp. Blinked sporadically as the room in which he slept appeared to him in a movement of spontaneous revelation. He considered the dream with his mind's eye. Nodding, he said out loud, "Yep. I reckon that's about right."

Chapter 22

November 22, 2000

Dear Alex,

It is midnight. The witching hour. For some reason I'll never understand, I always seem to become more lucid in the early morning hours. Now that I'm not socked out of my head with alcohol, that is. At any rate, I'm feeling better. So much so that I've decided to release myself from my current custodial situation. You're the first to know. I'll tell my good (?) doctor tomorrow.

Here's the situation. A few months ago, I decided to terminate my use of Aripiprazole. I became quite adept at feigning the swallowing of the pill and, sure enough, the old brain cleared remarkably. I look back on this two-year episode in the loony bin not as an ordeal to be scorned but as a necessary way station to sanity. As you know, I wasn't doing all that well in the outside world. To be honest, I was fucking up big time. But recently, something has happened to me. I don't know exactly what. But I have changed.

Since you're in Vermont, I thought I'd take up residence at our house in Homeland. What will I do, you ask? I don't rightly know. We'll see what happens.

So you've been chatting with Jane? I must say I always liked her. A little high strung but very kind. I don't know what to make of this whole Apollo/Dionysius dialectic that she has immersed herself in, but what the hell? It's a pleasant way to pass the time!

Oh, my, you've been drinking wine and contemplating the visions of Shakespeare. Good luck! But I must say I am intrigued by this whole notion of life being but a dream. However, I would say life is more of an apparition. Think on that my dear, philosophical brother.

Take care,
Raymond

Chapter 23

Alexander Lessing made a left out of his driveway and headed north on Snake Hollow Road. The sun had been up for a couple of hours, and the previous evening's snow lay across the countryside like a glistening, smooth, white blanket. Alex shifted into low gear to go up over a ridge, the chains on his tires holding fast to the snow-covered dirt road. Once over the ridge, he stayed in low gear so as not to have to apply the brakes going down into the shallow valley. Up ahead on the right, he perceived something incongruous in the pristine view. It wasn't that he detected something with his eyes. It was more that he observed something with his mind's eye. Something in the landscape was discordant. He didn't know *what* it was, but he knew *that* it was. He reflexively slowed down.

And then he saw it. A human arm. Attached to Blake Stallone's mailbox, next to Blake's driveway. The arm must have been secured to the top of the mailbox with some kind of superglue, because it stuck straight up into the air without any visible means of support. Had it been moving, it would have grotesquely mimicked some monstrous acknowledgment from the earth's mute core. But the arm was not moving. It was like a still, silent cipher announcing that everything familiar had ended. That nothing would ever be the same. The arm was encrusted with snow, but blood from the hacked off shoulder leaked through the snow and coagulated on the sides of the mailbox. The blood was more black than red, black like some pestilent bile from a diseased intestine.

Alex brought the truck to a stop. He stared through the passenger's side window at the severed arm. He stared at the gray fingers pointing skyward in rigor mortis as if suggesting that there were some answer to it all up there in the heavens.

Chapter 24

"I don't think this is a very good idea, Raymond."

"And why do you feel that way, Dr. Bevis?"

"I think you know why."

"I really don't. Please enlighten me."

"Because a balanced attack, with both medication and psychotherapy, is our best strategy."

"And what exactly are we attacking?"

"We're attacking your illness, Raymond. We're attacking the demons which brought you here."

"They're gone, Doc. There's nothing to attack."

"Now I'm aware of your progress. Don't get me wrong. But we have much more work to do."

"You know what I think, Doc? I think you're comfortable with our little routine. It's predictable and not entirely unpleasant. I think it suits your temperament."

"And what temperament is that?"

"Your need to feel in control. Your need to be dominant."

"Raymond, I think we should increase your medication just a tad and..."

"Forget it, Doc. I've made up my mind."

"Believe me when I tell you, Raymond, you're making a terrible mistake."

"Let me tell you the way I see it. You and I and everyone else who has ever existed on this planet have appeared within the realm of space and time without ever being consulted beforehand. No one has ever willingly been born. Hence, we find ourselves in a world where no one actually wants to be. Living this life is downright uncomfortable. And do you know why? Because we do not know what we're supposed to do! Sure, there are moral and cultural guidelines dictating how we are to behave. But if we're honest with ourselves, these guidelines drive us to lives of quiet desperation. Just read Freud's *Civilization and Its Discontents.* It's all there."

"Now, Raymond. With a slight increase in your medication..."

"And then there is death! What the hell is that all about? Let's see: we are unwillingly born into a world where we don't know what it is we're supposed to do, and no matter what we do, it doesn't seem to be quite right, and then we're told the next thing up on the hit parade is death!"

"You see, Raymond. We do have many more things to discuss..."

"You just don't get it, Doc. You can babble on until you're blue in the face about life and death and the meaning of it all, but what exactly do you accomplish? All you're doing is sending up smoke screens masking your own intellectual impotence."

"Raymond, I see that our time is up. I'd like you…"

"Doc, for once in your life, get real! Listen to me carefully. I'm releasing myself from this state of self-imposed institutionalization. I'm doing so because my mind is clear and I want very much to participate in this mad adventure into which I have unwillingly been born. You see, Doc, life is not going to wait for me to understand everything before I get my hands dirty. That's not what life does. It doesn't wait for anyone. It pushes you here and there and everywhere for its own sake—not for your sake or my sake, but its own sake. Life is all about the totality. We mistakenly think that life is about each one of us individually. We act as if life cares about what we want and what we need and what we must have! Nothing could be further from the truth. If your wants and needs are satisfied, it's not because of the power of your want or the power of your need. It's because what you wanted or needed happened to coincide with the grand plan of the totality."

"Raymond, we really must stop for today…"

"Doc, I wish you well. I really do. As for me, I'm going to leap into the great stream of life without any fear or remorse. I will navigate my life guided by the compass of my heart. Why? Because it strikes me as meaningful."

Chapter 25

Sheriff Rick Applegate and Deputy Sheriff Walt Dropo stood in the snow off to the side of Snake Hollow Road. Staring at the arm protruding from Blake Stallone's mailbox, they had been speechless for a good two minutes. Alex Lessing stood there with them. He too was speechless. The wind came up suddenly, whipping and howling throughout the hollow, causing the three men to tilt their bodies into the atmospheric maelstrom in order to maintain some semblance of balance.

Rick Applegate squinted into the whirlwind of snow. "We've got to go up to the trailer and see if Blake's okay. When I called earlier, he didn't answer the phone."

Walt nodded and began walking back to the police car.

"Where you going?" asked Rick.

Walt stopped and turned around. It felt to him as if time had stopped. He didn't like the feeling. "To the car. Ain't we goin' up to the trailer?"

Rick shook his head dismissively. "Walt, what you're going to do is take some photographs of that arm for the FBI." He winced in the windblown cold, his eyes tearing from the blustery snow raking across his face. "Then, take the godforsaken thing off the mailbox and put it in the trunk of the squad car."

Walt kicked the frozen ground, his surging rage causing him to stutter. "Wha'… wha'…"

"Just do it," said Rick. "Wrap the arm in the roll of plastic that's in the trunk." Rick circumnavigated the mailbox, studying the snow-covered ground. Then he stared at Blake's driveway disappearing into the woods. He turned to Alex. "Let's go to the trailer in your truck."

Alex and Rick hopped into the Dodge Ram pickup and headed up the driveway into the woods. Rick peered into the rearview mirror and observed Walt standing at the back of the police car. He looked like a wax figure that had no will of its own. "You know, Alex, I'm sure glad I'm sheriff."

"Why's that?"

"Because it means I'm not Walt."

Alex shook his head and smiled halfheartedly. He continued along the driveway and parked the truck in front of Blake Stallone's trailer. Switching off the engine, he acknowledged with a nod of his head Blake's Ford Bronco parked by the side of the trailer. "Looks like Blake's home," said Alex, his wavering voice betraying a sudden loss of hope.

Rick stared at the Bronco for what seemed to be too long. "I got a bad feeling about this."

Alex nodded. He was hardly breathing. "What do you want me to do?"

"I want you to stay right here." Rick squinted at the trailer through the gray, salt-dusted windshield, his eyes pointed in concentration. "You got a gun in the truck?"

Alex took a shallow breath. "No."

"All right. Just stay here." As if in slow motion, as if some invisible presence weighed heavily upon him, Rick opened the passenger's side door, climbed out of the truck, and shut the door behind him. The wind had died down and a steely silence permeated the scene. He studied the snow-covered ground in front of the trailer and then cast his gaze along the driveway.

Alex rolled down the driver's side window and leaned his head out. "What are you looking for?"

"Blood. I'm looking for blood. There's no blood here or in the driveway." In an almost detached kind of way, Rick reached down, unsnapped the flap on his holster, and retrieved his service revolver. He shook his head and mumbled to himself, "The snow could be covering it up."

"What?"

Rick didn't hear the question. He stood tall in the cold, silent white of the morning, his right arm hanging straight down at his side, his right hand deftly gripping the revolver. He raised his left arm to his head and secured his fur trooper's cap as if it were some kind of protective helmet.

Through the blurry, pockmarked windshield, Alex watched Rick disappear through the front door of the trailer. He sat there in the lingering cold, his mind frozen in some impenetrable quandary, time no longer passing, time no longer passing. In a spontaneous movement of fear, he climbed out of the truck.

Rick moved through the trailer with swift circumspection, surveying each room with a searching glance, revolver at the ready. There was nothing. No Blake. No evidence of a struggle. Nothing.

When Alex's legs gave way, he hit the frozen ground hard with his knees, the nausea washing over him.

Making a nervous clucking noise with his tongue, as if to signify that all was well, Rick strode back to the front door and out into the cold's dead calm. He stood in front of the trailer with apprehension, his eyes searching the landscape before him. His glance settled on the Dodge Ram pickup and the utter absence of Alex. Rick shook his head angrily and took off in a dead run around the side of the trailer, stopping abruptly when he saw the carnage. Alex was lying in the snow, his head in his hands, weeping. Rick swallowed hard, his legs turning to rubber as the horror rushed him in waves of nausea. Jagged chunks of bloody, mangled flesh and shards of sawed-off bones littered Blake's barbecue patio and fire pit. He couldn't distinguish the different parts of the body. There was no deciphering to be claimed. The wind picked up suddenly and whistled through the forest and made the trunks of the tall white birches sway to and fro like skeletons dancing to some black symphony eulogizing death and transfiguration.

Chapter 26

Aaron Riley cupped the evening grosbeak in the palm of his left hand. Sensing a surging power in the creature's stillness, he gently smoothed the black, brown, and white tail with the fingertips of his right hand. The finch looked at him with eyes that appeared to speak of thanksgiving, its pale greenish yellow bill opening and closing as if trying to talk. *There's nothin' to say, little bird,* thought Aaron. *You're better now, and it's time to return to the forest.* As if responding to Aaron's thoughts, the feathered being straightened up and commenced a stretching routine that announced it was preparing for flight. Aaron held his hand steady as the reborn creature fluttered its wings with purpose. And then it was up and away—circling majestically in the crisp, midday air some twenty feet above Aaron's head. Aaron watched the bird with reverence as it circled and dipped and circled and dipped like a ballerina in graceful farewell at the end of a poignant parting scene. Aaron breathed deeply and witnessed the grosbeak disappear into the surrounding evergreens. He cocked his head skyward and contemplated the clear, bright vastness—a vastness that made him think of what eternity must be like.

Chapter 27

Something was strange about the night sky blanketing the Elk Head Saloon. The moon and stars were out and clearly evident, and yet the light from those heavenly bodies was not gracing the earthly realm. Not tonight. Tonight was different. The cold was colder. The dark was darker. And everyone's heart was heavy.

Tonight at the Elk Head Saloon, the patrons weren't paying for their drinks. Jim Robertson, the owner of the saloon and a close friend of Blake Stallone, had declared a memorial evening in Blake's honor. All drinks were on the house.

Alex Lessing sat at the bar next to Alice Thornberry. He was deeply disturbed by Blake's untimely and appalling death, and the alcohol wasn't kicking in and working its magic as it usually did. Alex held his hands out in front of him just above the surface of the wooden bar. "They won't stop shaking, Alice. They've been shaking like this since early this morning."

Alice stared at his hands. "You're too young for your hands to shake like that."

Alex shrugged and shook his head. He felt like crying. "Christ, Alice, they don't *always* shake like that. It's just that I can't get out of my mind those godforsaken images of Blake's severed arm and his mutilated body."

Alice sipped her bourbon and pursed her lips. "I guess that *was* a terrible sight." Alice thought about Blake and what she had confided to him. Part of her was content with the fact that Blake had gone to his death with her confession. No leak was possible now. Another part of her missed him. After all, he had been a good friend and neighbor. Another part of her felt nothing. Alice wasn't surprised by anything anymore. She was too old for surprises.

Alex slugged down the last of his fourth beer and locked his shaking hands together. It struck Alice that he might be praying. Alex looked up toward the ceiling. Speaking to no one in particular, he said, "I'm getting the fuck out of here. I'm going as far away as I possibly can."

On a couple of barstools down from Alex and Alice sat Walt Dropo and Aaron Riley. Walt was drinking Bud Light from a silver aluminum can. Aaron was drinking Long Trail Ale from a pint glass with the word *Smuttynose* written in script across one side. Aaron studied Walt for a few moments, wondering why in the world Walt had taken up law enforcement for a living. "What I don't understand," said Aaron, "is why you stay in this job. You tell me that you hate goin' to work everyday and that you hate Rick Applegate, and yet you won't pull yourself together and do somethin' else."

Walt leaned his long, scrawny body forward, his sternum touching the front edge of the bar. His eyes were teary and bloodshot. "Aaron, I'm fifty years old, and I've always been a coward. I hate that about myself." He considered his can of Bud Light. He used to think Bud Light was his elixir. His liquid savior. *Shit, it's nothin' but piss water,* he thought. Walt turned his head and looked at Aaron. "You don't strike me as a coward, Aaron. No, sir. You strike me as somebody who takes head on whatever life throws at him." Walt sipped his beer. He could feel his brain melting down in an alcoholic daze. "I, on the other hand, am filled with fear. I'm pretty much fuckin' worthless."

Aaron took a swig of ale and gently placed the glass on the bar. "Walt, I want you to listen to me. Can you do that?"

Walt belched and nodded.

"I'm not gonna argue with you. If you tell me you're a coward and you're filled with fear, I'm gonna believe you. I'm takin' that as our startin' point."

Walt nodded, his eyes not quite focused.

"Walt, I think your problem is that you give your fear and cowardice too much strength. Okay, so you're fearful, you're cowardly. So be it. Let's get up and *act* anyway. Let's fully accept your fear and cowardice and get on with life in spite of it. You can do it that way. You can haul your fear and cowardice with you and still deal with life head on."

Walt screwed up his face and quizzically stared at Aaron. "You mean I can be a fuckin' coward and *still* stand up to Rick fuckin' Applegate?"

"Yeah. That's what I'm sayin'."

Walt stroked his smooth, freshly shaven chin. He felt the wheels of his brain chugging sluggishly in his cranium. "Now let me get this right. You're sayin' I can be a coward and *still* tell Rick fuckin' Applegate to go shit in his hat."

"That's what I'm sayin'." Aaron saw the need for further elaboration. "Walt, it's not your fault that you're a coward. Don't for one minute think that it is. You didn't choose to be this way. No, sir. Not at all. Whoever created this world *wants* you to be a coward."

Walt jutted out his jaw and cocked his head to the side. "What the fuck are you talkin' about?"

"Walt, you are who you are. You cannot be anyone other than yourself. So relax with that, accept it, and face life head on." Aaron looked around the barroom and saw Rick Applegate sitting at a corner table with Jim Robertson. He nodded toward the table. "There's Applegate. Over there with Jim. Go talk to him."

Walt squinted into the distance and belched loudly. He could feel his heart pounding erratically. "You know what? I'm gonna go up to Rick fuckin' Applegate and tell him I quit. Tell him I ain't takin' his shit no more. That's what I'm gonna tell him."

Aaron nodded and smiled. "Walt, if you quit your deputy job, I'll take you on as my assistant. You ever worked on transmissions?"

Walt was still squinting into the distance. He wasn't looking at anything in particular. Just kind of emptying his gaze into the void. "No. Never have. But I appreciate your offer." Walt pursed his lips and slid off the barstool. He hitched up his pants and headed off, swaggering unsteadily to and fro, toward Rick Applegate.

Aaron watched Walt negotiate about half the journey to the sheriff's table and then turned back to the bar. He was hoping against hope that things would work out for Walt. But he knew that hope wasn't enough. Everything had to line up just right for things to work out. Aaron slugged down the rest of his ale and looked up into the big, lazy, brown eyes of Madeline Kerr. "Hey, Maddy. Can you get me another?"

"Sure, Aaron." Maddy retrieved Aaron's glass, stepped up to the beer pulls, and drew another Long Trail Ale. She placed the cold, golden brown libation in front of Aaron and then leaned invitingly across the bar. "I saw you somewhere yesterday."

"You did?"

"Yep."

"Where?"

"At the Green Mountain Dharma Center."

Aaron raised his eyebrows suggestively. "Why didn't you come up and say hi?"

"Because you were busy. Meditating."

Aaron nodded nonchalantly. "Yeah. I go over and meditate a couple times a week."

Maddy wrinkled her freckled nose. "I was a bit surprised to see you over there. I didn't think you were interested in such things."

Aaron playfully squinted and pursed his lips. "Such as…?"

"You know, spirituality. Stuff like that."

Aaron laughed good-naturedly. "Everything is spiritual, Maddy. Even the stuff that appears to be purely physical."

Jim Robertson was behind the bar now. He gave Maddy a look that told her to get back to work. Maddy kindly nodded at Aaron. "I've got to get back. Could we talk again sometime?"

"Sure, Maddy. You know where to find me."

"Okay. Thanks."

Aaron smiled. He'd always liked Maddy. He hoped that she'd find whatever it was she was looking for. Aaron felt a presence hovering to the right of him and looked over. "Hey, Walt. How'd it go?"

Walt sat on the barstool next to Aaron and leaned his elbows on the bar. He seemed much more at ease. "Things are okay now between me and Rick."

Aaron enthusiastically clapped Walt on the shoulder. "Well, good for you, Walt. Good for you."

Walt nodded knowingly. "Yeah. I think we worked things out. Rick told me not to quit. He said if I wanted to make sheriff one day, I should just hang in there."

Aaron smirked. "Is that what you want, Walt? To be sheriff?"

Walt nodded. "Yeah. I think that would be okay."

"Hmmm. So what's the deal? Is Rick thinkin' of retirin'?"

Walt pondered the question, his brain slugging along in an alcohol-induced stupor. "You know, I'm not really sure. He didn't mention retirin' in so many words." Walt's eyes slowly moved side-to-side in their moist sockets. "But he did say I wouldn't have to wait long…until I could be sheriff."

"Hmmm." Aaron didn't know what to make of Walt's assessment. And he felt it wasn't the time to seek further clarification. "Well, Walt, I'm happy for you."

Walt smacked his lips. "Yeah. I think I'll be all right."

Rick Applegate staggered across the barroom and sat down next to Alice, who was still sitting by Alex. "Hey, Alice. Hey, Alex."

Alice and Alex nodded politely.

Alice rotated the glass of bourbon in her two gnarled, arthritic hands. She sat quietly, her beady eyes shifting back and forth. "How'd you know it was Blake?"

Rick turned his head toward Alice. "How'd I know what?"

"If his body was all chopped up, how'd you know it was Blake?"

Rick scratched his forehead. "We found his teeth. Took 'em to Doc Williams. They belonged to Blake."

Alice took a deep breath. "I see." She did see. Blake was gone. The one other soul on earth who knew her secret was gone. She stared into her glass of bourbon. *Sometimes the bad is not all bad*, she thought.

Chapter 28

Raymond Lessing sat at the large butcher-block table in the center of the massive kitchen in his Tudor-style home on Melrose Avenue in Baltimore's historic Homeland. He looked out of one of a series of tall, narrow windows into his sprawling yard, now dusted with snow. Squirrels were running around mischievously, like fiendish cartoon characters. He took a sip of coffee. Friendship Blend from the Baltimore Coffee and Tea Company. The smooth, nutty-vanilla flavor reminded him of Christmas eggnog shared with his classmates at Cal Tech. He listened to the silence of the big Tudor home, a home that his family had lived in for two generations, and found it to be quite edifying. It wasn't a silence that foretold impending loneliness. Rather, the silence spoke of spaciousness and freedom and a solitude in which one could ground oneself. He smiled and nodded within the silence and knew intuitively that he was all right. He knew that this time he would make a contribution to the world that would help inch it in the direction of sanctity. *After all, the world is sacred, is it not?* He scratched his head and smiled at the thought. How different he had become. This kind of thought was utterly new to him. And yet it formed in his mind with a natural spontaneity that was fortifying. He looked at the kitchen clock hanging on the wall: 8:00 a.m. Time was on his side. Or so it seemed. What would he do with all this time? What series of actions would he take to inch the world in the direction of sanctity? He contemplated the question and then allowed his mind to go blank. He lingered in that repose for a few moments and then witnessed, with some surprise, a communication of sorts being written across the screen of his consciousness. *Surrender to the mystery of life. Surrender to its native intelligence. Allow its energy to utilize your most creative proclivities to its own end. Questions paralyze those who think they are greater than the mystery. Effortless action is for those who abide in the mystery.*

Raymond awoke from the short but intense reverie and knew what he would do. He would hold himself out as a specialist in apparitional causation. He would share with the world his singular wisdom regarding the origin of the cosmos and its subsequent workings. After all, this kind of wisdom was essential for sane and proper conduct in one's life. He pulled a pen from the breast pocket of his flannel shirt and grabbed the pad of paper from the corner of the table. On the pad, he sketched out a rectangle in the shape of a business card. He paused for a moment, deep in thought. Then, with the grace and script of a calligrapher, he wrote in the center of the rectangle:

Raymond Lessing
SPECIALIST IN APPARITIONAL CAUSATION
What you don't know will hurt you!

Raymond smiled and put down his pen. He felt calm and collected. It felt good to know what he was supposed to do with his life.

Chapter 29

December 2, 2000

Dear Raymond,

In vino veritas. The damn, bloody truth! Ray, I'm drunk. Too much Pinot Noir. Too much of the damn, bloody truth! Yesterday, I discovered the chopped-up, mangled body of Blake Stallone scattered across his back patio. A madman had taken a chainsaw to him. It was just plain horrible. Needless to say, I've had it! I'm done! To be honest, I make myself sick. I'm so tired of wandering around in a fog of subterfuge—looking here, there, and everywhere for self-enhancement! We (the human race) are a grave disappointment. If there is a God...well, let's not go there.

I've made a decision. I'm going away. Far away. Indonesia. To hell with the book on ethics. God, what was I thinking? Can I honestly hold myself out as a specialist in ethics? I've been such a fool! At any rate, I'm going to Bali. I'm going to study Buddhism. No, I'm going to live Buddhism! When I'm settled, I'll send you a forwarding address. We must continue to write.

Your brother who has forgotten how to laugh,
Alex

Chapter 30

Rick Applegate dabbed at a ketchup stain on his dark blue tie with a graying napkin that he had retrieved from a grease-soaked McDonald's hamburger bag. After treating his tie, he got up from behind his desk and looked out the window onto Jefferson Street. It was unspeakably cold. Six degrees Fahrenheit. For three o'clock in the afternoon, it was extraordinarily quiet. The street was empty save for two old men in their heavy parkas, sitting on lawn chairs, smoking cigars out in front of Duke Spencer's hardware store. Rick stared at the old codgers and wondered what it must be like to be that old. Wondered what it must be like to have seen and endured so many of life's incessant oddities. Rick shook his head, and a sad smile slowly appeared across his forlorn face. *They sure seem to be enjoying their cigars,* he thought. *At least that's something.*

Rick looked about the empty office, nodded knowingly, and walked through the office into the adjoining room that led to the cells in the back. Stopping at the gun cabinet, the sheriff selected the correct key off his key chain and unlocked the cabinet door. He noticed how calm he was. By all rights, he shouldn't be. But he was. He pulled a Remington Model 870P shotgun off the rack, placed the butt of the rifle on the floor, and leaned the barrel up against his right leg. After carefully resecuring the cabinet, he grabbed the rifle and walked across the room to the ammunition drawer. The ammunition drawer.

That's what they called it. Just the top drawer of an old metal desk that they kept locked. He leaned the rifle up against his leg as he had before. The parkerized metal finish of the barrel was ice cold, and the chill bled through his pant leg like a premonition of death. He opened the drawer and retrieved a box of 2¾-inch twelve-gauge shells. After selecting two shells from the box and putting them in the breast pocket of his shirt, he returned the box to the drawer and locked it away. He picked up the rifle, walked back into the office, laid the weapon down on top of his desk, and returned to the window looking out onto Jefferson Street. The two old men were still sitting there smoking their cigars. The smoke pluming over their heads was indistinguishable from the carbon dioxide escaping from their dry mouths. Rick contemplated lighting up a cigar but then thought better of it. *No point in stinking up the office.* He glanced one last time at the cigar smokers, pulled the two twelve-gauge shells out of his shirt pocket, and turned away from the window.

The explosion was loud enough to be heard outside. Loud enough to be heard across the street. But no one heard it. No one was about except the two old men smoking cigars, and their hearing was long gone. When the shot rang out, one of the old men was telling the other about the time last summer when he and his black lab, Gus, were down at the sugarhouse drinking rum. "Yep," the old man said, "Gus likes drinkin' rum." The other old man smiled and nodded, not hearing a word his friend had said.

Chapter 31

The night sky was cloud covered and the darkness unforgiving. Madeline Kerr drove her pickup east on Route 4 and made a right onto an unmarked dirt road that was immediately swallowed up by a forest of evergreens. She flicked on her high beams, but the black stands of spruce and pine ominously leaned into her like the narrow walls of an abandoned tunnel. About a mile into the evergreens, the forest thicket opened up to a hilly terrain of white poplars. Off in the distance, she could see a halo of yellow light hovering like a beacon of hope around a solitary log cabin. When she pulled up in front of the cabin, her high beams slashed across its porch, revealing Aaron Riley standing at the top of the steps, cigar in one hand, a lowball tumbler cradling some golden liquid in the other. Madeline shifted the truck into PARK, grabbed her book off the passenger's seat, and hopped out.

Aaron nodded as an inviting smile appeared spontaneously across his big, bearded face. "Hey, Maddy. Did you have any trouble findin' the place?"

"No trouble at all, Aaron." She stopped several yards in front of the porch steps and gazed contemplatively at the log cabin. "Did you build this cabin?"

"Sure did."

"It's beautiful."

Aaron nodded shyly. "Come on in. It's colder than a witch's tit out here."

Madeline snickered at Aaron's colorful language and walked up the porch steps and into the cabin. A fire was blazing in a black iron potbelly stove in one corner of the cozy living area. The odor of cedar flowered in the air. Madeline surveyed the log walls. "Are the logs made of cedar?"

"Yeah. Northern white cedar from Maine."

"I love the smell of cedar."

"Me too." Aaron placed his drink on a cherry coffee table in the center of the room and leaned his cigar in the clay ashtray sitting on the table. "Let me help you with your coat."

"Thanks. I appreciate that," said Madeline, slipping off her heavy, insulated ski jacket. She liked the gentle touch of Aaron's big hands on her shoulders.

Aaron took the coat, walked over to the dining area, and draped it over the back of a straight-backed, wooden chair. He looked up and saw Madeline studying the layout of the place. "This is really nice," said Madeline. "Everything is right here in one room."

"Yeah. For a single guy like me, it's perfect. I built it so that my kitchen and dinin' room and livin' room would just kind of flow into one another." Aaron paused and motioned with his hand to an alcove off to the side of the kitchen. "And then I got my bedroom and bathroom back there."

Madeline smiled and looked around the room once again. "Yeah. I really do like it."

Aaron looked at the book in Madeline's hand and began to approach her. "What have you got there?"

Madeline smiled, a bit embarrassed. "Oh, it's a book I want to show you. It's a book on Zen Buddhism."

Aaron nodded and held out his hand. "Okay, let's have a look."

Madeline handed him the book and watched him carefully examine both the front and back covers. "Hmmm," said Aaron. "Why are you interested in Zen?"

"Oh, it's kind of a crazy story."

"Is this what you wanted to talk to me about? Zen?"

Suddenly Madeline felt unsure of herself. She felt unsure about everything having to do with meeting Aaron like this. She spoke hesitantly. "Well, yes. I hope you don't mind."

Aaron smiled softly, the corners of his eyes crinkling mischievously. "No problem. But first, I'd like you to try some of my homemade moonshine."

Madeline burst out laughing. She felt at once happy and relieved.

"Did I say somethin' funny?" asked Aaron.

"No. Just get me some of that moonshine. I've got a feeling I'm going to need it."

Aaron raised his eyebrows and nodded. "So be it."

Chapter 32

Walt Dropo stood, hands on hips and heart pounding hard, beneath the bright fluorescent lights of the sheriff's office. The smell of ammonia was oppressive and conjured thoughts of death and what may lie beyond. He looked at his watch: 10:00 p.m. The janitorial crew was finishing up. Except for the smell, no one ever would have known that anything untoward had happened here today, that Rick Applegate's brains had been splattered across the wall behind his desk like a catapulted bowl of red chili. Walt walked over to his own desk and sat on the front edge. He stared down at his brown, scuffed hiking boots. *What a fuckin' mess,* he thought. *Rick told me I wouldn't have long to wait to be sheriff. He fuckin' told me. But I wasn't expectin' this. No, sir. Not this.*

"Mr. Walt? Mr. Walt?"

Walt looked up. "Yeah?"

"We're finished cleanin' up."

Walt nodded.

"We're real sorry about what happened to Mr. Rick."

Walt nodded.

"So we'll be goin' now."

"Okay."

The janitors closed the office door behind them, leaving Walt sitting on the edge of his desk contemplating his boots. Walt looked up and surveyed the office. He had never seen it like this before. Everything was surrealistically clear and sharply defined. And the silence was deafening. As if he were twenty feet beneath the surface of a still lake. He raised himself from his desk and walked over to Rick's. He stared at the wooden surface, no longer smooth. It had a gritty stain of colorless gray about it, but at least it was no longer mottled by the shades of Rick's blood and tissue. The coroner had said Rick took the blast in his mouth. Walt thought about that. *He stuck that fuckin' shotgun in his mouth!* Suddenly, Walt spasmodically doubled over. He was fighting for breath, fighting against the swarming brainstorm of thoughts and images rising to the surface of his consciousness. Finally, the attack subsided. Walt stood up, a little woozy, and rubbed his face with the palms of his hands. *I gotta suck it up. No time for self-pity. I'm sheriff now.* Walt sighed deeply and established his bearings. He plodded back to his desk, grabbed his coat off the back of his chair, and slipped it on. He turned the lights off on his way out.

The former deputy stood in the dark in front of the office and looked up and down Jefferson Street. Not a living creature to be seen. Not even a dog or cat or rat. In the godforsaken cold, he looked up and down the street for nearly a quarter of an hour. Then he spat in the gutter and walked away.

Chapter 33

Maddy sipped Aaron's homemade moonshine. The golden brown libation burned going down but then softened with the finish. "This is good," she said hoarsely.

Aaron smiled sheepishly. "It's one of my better batches. I blend it with wheat instead of rye. That's what makes it so smooth."

"You're quite the Renaissance man, aren't you?"

"Oh, I wouldn't say that. I live a simple life. I'm not into complication and fanfare. Just pretty much keep to myself."

Maddy sat quietly next to Aaron on his black leather couch. The warmth of the fire bathed her in what seemed like serenity. She looked at the book Aaron had consigned to the coffee table in front of them. "So tell me about your experiences at the Green Mountain Dharma Center."

Aaron shrugged his massive shoulders. "There's not much to tell. I just go over there and meditate."

"What got you into meditation?"

Aaron looked at her, wondering how much he should reveal about himself. "Maddy, let me ask you a question. Exactly how serious are you about developin' spiritually?"

Maddy was surprised by the question. She didn't really know the answer.

Aaron continued, "Let me just say this. The spiritual path is all or nothin'. There ain't no half way. If you're really interested in learnin', I can help you. Otherwise, let's just hang out and enjoy each other's company." He took a swig of bourbon and leaned his head back, enjoying his comforts and her company to his heart's content.

Chapter 34

Matt Lawlor slammed the cell door and stepped back quickly. He pensively studied the prisoner, staring at him through the steel bars of the cage. He'd never seen one like him before. This one didn't seem to feel the cold or pain or anything. This one seemed hardly human. His eyes held the mystery. Black eyes. Eyes like scratched glass. Whatever was behind those eyes was dead. Nothing resembling life at all. Just cold stillness that extended forever and ever into some internal black and soulless void. The eyes were what gave Matt Lawlor the willies. Not to mention that the prisoner had only one arm.

Chapter 35

Raymond Lessing shivered as he pulled up the collar of his leather bombardier jacket. The wind had picked up and was driving an icy stake through his torso. It was noon and the sun was out, but the cold was relentless. He stood on the corner of Charles and Centre Streets, right outside the Walters Art Museum, just south of the Washington Monument. The lunchtime crowd filtered through the streets of downtown Baltimore, and everyone who passed within arm's length of Raymond received his newly minted *Specialist in Apparitional Causation* business card. Most of the streaming passersby stuck the cards into their overcoat pockets and continued on their ways. A few tossed the cards into the street gutter. Nobody actually took the time to look at it. After an hour of this exercise in futility, Raymond, as if pulled by some cosmic magnet, walked north on Charles Street, up the hill past the towering obelisk, across the cobbles of Monument Street, and for another block until he arrived at the Brass Elephant Restaurant. He stopped suddenly at the foot of the establishment's marble steps.

Raymond stared at the ornate doorway and considered what he might do. The Elephant was not a place that conjured up entirely good memories. In fact, it was the last place he had got drunk before ending up at Sheppard Pratt. He looked up to the second floor of the building and stared at the stained glass windows. The Tusk Lounge. That was where the medics had picked him up and carried him out. He could still hear somewhere in the caverns of his consciousness the echo of his own wailing.

His throat was suddenly dry, and the wind kicked up in a strange vortex that drew aloft whatever trash lined the gutters. The amalgam of paper and plastic and Styrofoam whirled like a disembodied dervish in a kaleidoscopic dance of chaos. With openness to an uncertain future, Raymond surrendered to the moment, trudged up the restaurant's marble steps, pulled open the heavy iron and glass door, and entered the comely foyer. An elegantly dressed man in his late sixties, with graying hair and a pencil-thin mustache, stood behind a grand, delicately carved lectern, meticulously reviewing the restaurant's reservation log. His dignified air resembled that of a British butler.

Somewhat breathless, Raymond approached the butler. "Excuse me. Is Edward in today?"

The fastidious steward looked up from the reservation log, his severely pointed nose angling auspiciously toward the heavens. His eyes were cold and gray and distant. He spoke softly, as if it were an unwelcome strain on his otherwise pleasant existence. "If you are referring to Mr. Darby, you are well advised to make yourself present in the Tusk Lounge." The butler retrieved an elaborate gold fob from the inside pocket of his silk suit jacket and quickly glanced at the antique timepiece attached. "Twelve fifteen. Mr. Darby has a martini in the Tusk Lounge at precisely twelve fifteen."

Staring at the fussy compulsive, Raymond nodded. He wasn't feeling so good, engulfed in a state of mild terror laced with a dash of entropy. "Thanks. I'll go up and see him." Raymond lugged his heavy legs down the hall, passing by a variety of elegant elephant sconces to which the restaurant owed its name. He made a hard left and hauled his way up the two steep flights of stairs to the entrance of the Tusk Lounge. When he reached the top landing, he felt better. *What a difference a minute or two makes,* he thought. *The mind fades in and out of terror with no rhyme or reason.*

Raymond entered the lounge with circumspection. The back bar directly in front of him was brightly lit. The colorful bottles, housing multifarious nectars of transcendence, sparkled like the dancing lights of a summer night's carnival. Raymond's gaze gravitated to the right. Sitting alone at a table in the corner, sipping a Beefeater martini, was Edward Darby. Edward was hunched over the table, reading the *City Paper.*

"What are you reading?"

"An article on John Waters," Edward mumbled. "He's one crazy fucker." He sipped his martini and looked up. "Well, I'll be damned!"

"Hi, Edward."

"Hello, Raymond! Hello! What a pleasant surprise!" Edward leaped up from the table, walked briskly to Raymond's side, and warmly shook his old friend's hand. "My, my. Catch me up on things, Raymond!"

Raymond shrugged impishly. "Well, I'm out of the loony bin."

"I can see that." Edward beamed at Raymond, his clean-shaven, cherubic face brightly reflecting the light show from the back bar. "Hey, can I get you a martini?"

"No, thanks. I'm good."

"Well, come and sit down. Let's catch up." Edward slung his arm over Raymond's shoulder and led him to the corner table. The two men sat down and stared fondly at one another in silence. Edward couldn't stop smiling. He really liked Raymond. Always had. He eyed Raymond cautiously. "How was the loony bin? Your words, not mine."

"In an odd way, it served a much-needed purpose."

"How so?"

"I found out what I'm supposed to do."

Edward squinted. "What you're *supposed* to do?" Edward didn't like such dramatic proclamations. He was more of a freethinking bon vivant.

"Yeah. It came to me in a series of dreams."

"Dreams? What kind of dreams?"

Raymond smiled and leaned over the table. "The thing about the loony bin is that you can't dream if you're on drugs. The drugs shut down the mind. You can't dream. Hell, you can't even think."

Edward raised one eyebrow. He seriously wondered if Raymond were abusing drugs at that moment.

"The drugs will make you hallucinate. But they won't allow you to dream."

Edward sucked on his martini. "Are you talking about dreaming when you're asleep?"

"Yeah. Dreaming when you're asleep."

Edward sighed. "Go on."

"You see, they had me on some heavy antidepressants. It was like living in a fog. But I prevailed. I became very adept at lodging the pills between my cheek and gum as I swallowed the accompanying water." Raymond looked around the empty Tusk Lounge as if he were checking for eavesdroppers. "It took about two months to extricate myself from the fog. But when I did, I started to dream."

Edward scratched his head. He didn't know where Ray was going with this. "Go on."

"Did you know that the mind has the capacity to act like an electronic receiver? Did you know that? Well, it does. And do you know who transmits the messages to the receiver? God!" Raymond pursed his lips and squinted. "In my dreams, God transmitted to me a full-blown scientific theory about the first cause of the cosmos and all subsequent transformations thereafter." Raymond reached into his coat pocket, pulled out a business card, and slid it across the table.

Edward stared at the card.

Raymond Lessing
SPECIALIST IN APPARITIONAL CAUSATION
What you don't know will hurt you!

Edward looked up, confused and dismayed. "So you're a specialist in apparitional causation?"

Raymond nodded. "That I am." He wrinkled his nose. "That's what I'm here on earth to do. To spread the word about apparitional causation."

Edward swilled down the remainder of his martini. He felt short of breath. "Do you think there's much of an audience for this...this *special* theory?"

Raymond's eyes glassed over. "Edward, it may be the most important theory ever to grace the earthly realm." Raymond sat quietly for a moment. "But I'm really not sure if anyone is ready to hear it. It kind of turns everything upside down."

Edward shook his head dismissively. "People don't want their world turned upside down, Ray. They like things right side up. They like the status quo." Edward gazed at his empty martini glass. "I like knowing that at precisely twelve fifteen in the afternoon, I am going to sip a Beefeater martini in the solitude of the Tusk Lounge. It keeps my world on an even keel. It gives me a sense of solidity."

Raymond opened his eyes wide. "But, Edward, it's of the utmost importance that the theory of apparitional causation be dispersed far and wide. The knowledge this theory reveals changes the entire landscape of wisdom. We cannot lead sane lives without this knowledge."

Edward sank his chin into the palm of his left hand. He looked out onto the bright, shining countenance of the Tusk Lounge with forlorn eyes and an uneasy conscience. "Where's Alex? Are you living with him?"

"Alex is in Indonesia. Trying to find himself. He wants to be a Buddhist."

Edward shook his head. "Good Lord," he mumbled.

"What's that?"

"I said, 'good for him.'"

"Hmmm. I'm living at the house in Homeland."

"Good." Edward concentrated his attention. "Look, Ray. There's a club of sorts that meets here in the Tusk Lounge every Thursday at midnight. I think they may have some interest in your theory."

"What kind of club?"

"Well, I guess it's more like a society than a club. They call themselves the Baltimore League of Disenfranchised Thinkers."

Raymond leaned back in his chair. He could feel his heart palpitating. "Hmmm. What makes you think they'd be interested in my theory?"

Edward shrugged and gazed at Raymond. "I'm not going to lie to you. This is one weird-ass group. I'm just saying that I think they would be interested."

"I hesitate to unveil my theory on deaf ears."

Ray's failure to see the forest for the trees cast Edward into a quiet funk. He smiled halfheartedly. "I think you'll have to talk to those who are willing to listen. I don't think you have the luxury of being selective."

Raymond looked up at the ceiling as if searching for guidance. "All right. I'll speak to them."

Edward took a deep breath. "Good, Ray. Good for you."

Chapter 36

Walt Dropo sipped his black coffee and stared out the window onto Jefferson Street. It was the second week of December, and the cold bored itself deeply into the collective membrane of all that lived. Ever since Rick died, the cold seemed colder. At least it seemed that way to Walt. No explaining it, really. The truth was Walt just couldn't get warm. A permanent chill had calcified in the marrow of his bones. Walt pursed his lips and turned away from the window. He walked slowly to his desk and sat behind it. He stared down at the scrubbed, gray, wooden surface of the desk. The surface that had had remnants of Rick's face smeared over it. Walt shook his head and blinked away some tears. It was damn quiet in the sheriff's office. Damn quiet. But then, out of the depths of stillness, came the shrill peal of the black phone sitting on the desk.

Walt leaned forward, picked up the phone, and brought it to his ear. "Sheriff's office."

There was a long silence on the other end of the line. "Is this Sheriff Dropo?"

Walt swallowed hard. "Yeah, it is. What can I do for you?"

"This is Sheriff Matt Lawlor. Down in Albany."

Walt held the phone in silence, as if he were mute.

"Hey, I'm sorry about what happened to Rick."

Walt winced. "Yeah, we're all sorry. But life goes on. At least, that's what they say."

"Yeah. Life goes on. That's for sure." Dead air. "Hey, look. A couple of nights ago, one of our state troopers apprehended a drifter who had stolen a car. Pulled him over on Route 87. We locked him up here in Albany for safekeepin'. When we ran a background check on him, the sky fell in. We're pretty damn sure he killed Blake Stallone."

Walt could feel his heart pounding like a jackhammer. "No kiddin'?"

"Yeah. This fucker is buckin' for psycho of the century. He's got a grisly rap sheet. In and out of prison his whole life. Just finished servin' ten years for armed robbery."

"What's this have to do with Blake?"

"Blake shot him ten years ago. Blew his left arm apart with a Remington 870 pump shotgun. The wound trauma was so bad, the doctors couldn't save it."

"Oh, shit." In his mind's eye, Walt could see Blake's arm pointing skyward from the mailbox. It was his left arm.

Matt Lawlor sucked at his back right molar. It had been hurting him for a while now. He cradled the phone and spoke in a whisper. "The thing is, Walt, this fucker ain't right. I don't know how to describe it. There's somethin' about him that I ain't never seen before. He's got dead man's eyes."

Walt felt the skin on his face go numb. "What's dead man's eyes?"

Matt rubbed his chapped lips with the back of his hand. "You gotta see 'em to understand."

Walt sadly looked down and stared into the emptiness of the scrubbed desk top.

"The thing is, Walt, I'm gonna have to transfer him up to you for the murder trial. You're the lucky one with jurisdiction."

Walt felt his brain searching for something to say. "Did he confess?"

"What?"

"Did he confess to Blake's murder?"

Matt chuckled soberly. "He ain't said a word since he got here. He don't talk. He don't eat. He don't sleep. He hardly breathes. I'll be fuckin' glad to get rid of him."

"So he didn't confess?"

"He killed Blake. Believe me."

Walt felt his jaw stiffen. "Yeah. I know he did."

"I'll fax you down a full report in a couple days."

Walt sat still and quiet. It was as if time were a brick wall, and Walt had hit it head on and in full force. "Matt?"

"Yeah?"

"Why do you say he's got dead man's eyes?"

Silence. "'Cause there ain't nobody alive behind 'em."

Recoiling involuntarily, Walt winced and his mouth twisted to the side. All he managed to say was, "Thanks for callin', Sheriff."

"Sure thing."

Walt hung up the phone. He raised himself from his chair and walked over to the window. He stared out onto Jefferson Street. A cold, gray shadow stretched lengthwise along the street like a gangplank walked by the souls of the dead. A few people were milling about, but Walt didn't see them. He stared through them as if they were ghosts out of some forgotten past. What Walt saw was a reflection inside his mind. A reflection of a future that he prayed would never arrive.

Chapter 37

December 22, 2000

Dear Ray,

The Hindu Yogis believe that a specific phrase or sentence spoken at just the right time to one who is receptive and ready can bring about instantaneous illumination. Perhaps our written words can function in this way. Perhaps they can become instruments of grace.

I have much to tell you about my new life here in Bali. To put it simply, I'm in no man's land. In Bali, nothing is recognizable to me, least of all myself. Everything is a jolt to my sensibilities. The colors, sounds, tastes, and smells are foreign to me. I have no concepts with which to frame my experiences. Like you and your recent release from Sheppard Pratt, I don't know how this will turn out.

Ray, you and I see a distant shore. A shore beyond madness. It is the only refuge worth living (and suffering!) for. The irony is that we must pass through the madness to arrive at the shore lying beyond. Once you're in the center of the maelstrom, there is no turning back. We must go all the way through the madness and rise up from the shattered remains of what we once called the self. The shards of the false self must be left in the rubble.

Whatever pure and subtle energy is left over must then gather itself anew on the distant shore.

Poor Dr. Bevis has no clue. He wants to lift you out of the rubble and glue you back together with chemical compounds. But the glue won't hold. It never does. And I, my dear brother, have mainlined the drug of academia for my fraudulent makeover. It too will not work. It too will not hold. The shattered self must be abandoned.

I live in a cave at the Goa Gaja Temple. Goa Gaja lies between the cities of Ubud and Mas. The temple is inhabited by Hindu and Buddhist monks, some of whom are very old and transcendent—they are the ones who have gone beyond madness to the other shore. I live the simple life of a renunciate. All of us here are either traversing the ocean of madness or have reached the shore beyond. Unlike your custodians at Sheppard Pratt, my keepers don't want to glue me back together. They are calmly waiting for me to shatter into pieces. On the other side of madness is the quiet shore of peace.

You may write to me c/o General Post Office, Ubud, Bali, Indonesia.

Your humble brother,
Alex

Chapter 38

Alice Thornberry clutched her glass of I.W. Harper in hands wearing thin wool gloves with the fingertips cut off. The bitter cold of central Vermont on this Christmas night was nothing short of glacial. But that didn't keep the Elk Head Saloon faithful from braving the elements. Even if some of them had to wear gloves inside the cozy establishment.

Aaron Riley pushed up the brim of his red Budweiser ball cap and stared down at Alice. He looked like some humanoid mountain sitting next to Alice's worn, hunched-over body. "Did you hear they found out who killed Blake?"

Alice looked up. Her beady eyes darted back and forth. "No. I didn't hear nothin' about it."

"Yeah. Walt got a call from the sheriff down in Albany. State police caught a guy on Route 87 who stole a car in Rutland. When they ran a background check on him, they figured he was the one who killed Blake."

Alice shook her head, wondering if there were any rhyme or reason for anything anymore. "How'd they figure that?"

"They put two and two together."

Alice smiled wryly. She cocked her frail, bony head to the side. "Why are you fuckin' with me, Aaron?"

Aaron leaned over and gave Alice a one-armed bear hug. She screamed and wriggled like a little girl. He then leaned back and shook his head. "I don't mean to make fun of Blake's death or anything like that. It's just that this whole story is so weird."

Alice sipped her I.W. Harper. She pursed her lips in contemplation. "You know, Aaron, a lot of weird shit is happenin' around here lately. I wonder what that's all about?"

Aaron took a deep draw of Bass Ale. He looked up at the sparkling white Christmas lights decorating the back bar. "Life has always been strange. That's its nature. When all this weird shit hits you at once, that's when you notice it."

Alice smirked. "Maybe so." She jabbed Aaron's arm with her pointy elbow. "So tell me about puttin' two and two together."

"As it turns out, Blake had shot this guy some ten years ago. The wound was so bad, the perp lost his left arm."

Alice turned her face toward Aaron and squinted at him. "Blake didn't seem the kind to shoot somebody."

Aaron nodded. "I guess it all depends on the circumstances." Aaron returned his attention to his beer. He sat quietly. He smiled internally. He could feel Alice getting impatient.

"Well, go on! Tell me what happened!"

Aaron nodded. "Apparently, this lunatic was robbin' a deli in Brooklyn. One of the clerks pressed the silent alarm that notifies the cops."

Alice scratched the side of her nose with her gloved hand, her eyes signaling some inner quandary. "I thought Blake was in homicide. Why would he get the call?"

Aaron laughed wryly. "You're a sly one, Alice. You make a good point. That's part of what makes this story so strange. On that particular day, Blake's car had broken down, and he was makin' his rounds with a uniformed patrolman in a squad car. When the emergency call came in, they were right in the area."

Alice cocked her head and pursed her lips. "Okay. Go on."

"The perp had taken a butcher knife from the deli and was threatenin' the patrons. Apparently, he wanted to rape a young girl in front of her mother."

Alice screwed up her face and snorted. "Crazy fucker."

"Yeah. That's for sure. Anyway, one of the clerks broke free and was runnin' down the street tryin' to escape. The maniac got pissed and went after her with the butcher knife."

Alice's jaw tightened. "And Blake was waitin' for him."

"Yup. Blake shot him."

"And blew off his left arm."

"Yup."

"And now the bastard came back to take Blake's left arm."

"Yup."

"And that's how you put two and two together?"

"Yup."

Alice slugged down the last of her I.W. Harper. She stared at the back bar aimlessly. "Sometimes I wonder if this life ain't some big fuckin' joke."

Aaron nodded silently.

"I'm goin' home now."

"Okay, Alice. Merry Christmas to you."

"And to you." Alice climbed down off the barstool and shuffled her way toward the coatrack over by the front door of the saloon.

Aaron watched Alice as she meandered through the boisterous crowd of holiday drinkers. Then he turned around and was met by the chocolate brown eyes of Maddy Kerr. Maddy slid another pint of Bass Ale under Aaron's nose. "A Christmas present from me."

Aaron nodded. "That's mighty kind of you." He paused and looked at her smiling face. "You off New Year's Eve?"

Maddy winked at him coyly. "I am."

"You wanna come out to the cabin?"

"Yes. That would be nice." Maddy smiled and nodded. "I've been thinking about what you said. About the spiritual life. I think I would like to learn from you."

Aaron stared down into his frothy, brown libation. The head looked like a thick cumulus cloud. He looked up at Maddy. "Do you remember what I said? It's all or nothin'."

A pall of serious consternation fell across Maddy's face like a slowly moving shadow. "I remember. All or nothing."

Aaron nodded. "Okay then."

~ ~ ~ ~ ~

Alice Thornberry walked among the dark, long-lying shadows of the parking lot in front of the Elk Head Saloon. A strange, silver fog had settled in the valley like a curtain of ice. Searching for her keys, she stopped momentarily in front of her Jeep and did not notice next to it the dark figure of a man sitting in a rusted-out Pontiac Bonneville. She secured her car key, scrambled up into her Jeep, turned the ignition, and drove off.

Walt Dropo watched the Jeep disappear into the night's arctic black. He shivered in the oppressive cold and blew on his hands, his cheeks taut from the tears that had frozen there. He looked down at the open straight razor lying on the passenger's seat. Stared at it for the hundredth time. Searched for and found his pulse on his left wrist. His heart was beating. He could feel it in his wrist. But he didn't feel alive. What he felt was fear. The kind of fear that dragged him down into the bowels of some uncharted dimension between life and death. Death. That would be a better place to be. A place outside of fear's disabling clutches. It would only take a second. One second. And he would be on the way to death.

From some internal corridor of depression, Walt watched himself pick up the straight razor. Watched the blade gleam supernaturally in the utter lack of light. Walt thought to himself: *What did Aaron say? You can be fearful and still act? Be fearful and still meet life head on?* Walt swallowed hard and shook his head dismissively. *I'm nothin' but a fuckin' coward. Can't do one simple thing. Not one simple thing.*

Chapter 39

Raymond Lessing stood with pointed anticipation in the shadow-laden hallway outside the Tusk Lounge. He could hear voices, subdued and secretive, on the other side of the wall. He looked at his watch. Two minutes past midnight. Downstairs, the Brass Elephant was closed for the evening. Edward Darby had let him in and told him to go upstairs. The League of Disenfranchised Thinkers was anxious to meet him. As for Edward, he was headed to the Marble Bar at the Belvedere Hotel for a little drinking with the culinary vampires.

To be the bearer of a life-altering message is no small responsibility, thought Raymond. He swallowed hard and rolled his shoulders as if he were preparing for some physically demanding challenge. Then, out of some timeless space, he felt a heavy hand on his shoulder.

"Good evening, my friend," said a disembodied voice.

Raymond slowly turned around and was accosted by the curvature of the largest head he had ever seen. "Good evening," said Raymond, reflexively leaning away from the overbearing cranium.

The large head smiled, its elongated mouth curling across its wide face like a twisted river. "Actually, if we are to be precise, our greeting should be 'good morning.'"

Raymond nodded. *Sure. Whatever.*

"Allow me to introduce myself," said the large head. "I am Henry Appletree. I am a solipsist."

Raymond felt a spasm in the muscles at the back of his neck. "Uh...I'm Raymond Lessing."

"And...you're a...?" asked the large head, its saucer-like eyes sparkling intensely.

Raymond felt his mouth go dry. And, to make matters worse, he had a sudden urge to urinate. "Uh...Uh...I'm an apparitional causationist."

The big head cocked itself to the side. "Hmmm. Very interesting." The head nodded what was perhaps a vague sign of approval. "Well, we always welcome a new voice to the chorus."

Raymond felt a clammy splash of perspiration trickle down the back of his neck. "I'm going to use the bathroom. Then I'll be in to meet the rest of the group." Raymond pushed past the imposing head and walked quickly down the hall. After locking the lavatory door and judging the barricade sufficient, he relaxed and relieved himself. He washed his hands at the sink and stood staring at himself in the mirror. He regarded his aging face. The graying hair at his temples. The dark circles beneath his glassed-over eyes. For the briefest of moments, he thought of escaping down the back stairway. After all, the stairs were right outside the bathroom. But then he reconsidered. *What is important is the message. I am only the messenger. Perhaps I am the **only** messenger.* Feeling a renewed sense of worthiness,

Raymond smiled at himself in the mirror and returned to the somber hallway leading to the interlocutors' den.

The Tusk Lounge was cast in dark shadows, and save the halogen lighting from behind the bar, it was uncomfortably bleak. In the back corner, two round tables were pushed together, each arrayed with but a squat, flickering candle centered precisely. Four blob-like men in colorless sweaters hunched around the tables and over drinks, talking in low and hushed tones. The macabre forms eclipsing the wall behind them conjured up unwanted visions of the grotesque. The projected shape of Mr. Appletree's head loomed like a giant carnivorous mushroom about to devour its prey. In spite of these inauspicious circumstances, Raymond the messenger was not to be deterred.

A voice materialized from behind the bar. "Good to see you, Ray. It's been a while."

Raymond turned and was happy to see a familiar face. Rick Irvin. Long-time barkeep at the Tusk Lounge. "Hey, Rick. Good to see you, too."

Rick pulled down a tumbler from the rack above his head. "Still drinking the usual?"

Raymond smiled and shook his head. "No. I'll just have club soda with lime."

"Coming up, my friend."

Raymond's gaze drifted back to the four blobs in the corner. Out of the flickering gray gloom, he felt them staring at him.

Not without expectation. *Perhaps they can sense the power and sanctity of the message,* thought Raymond.

The giant head stood up and welcomed Raymond with an awkward movement of his arm. "Raymond, allow me to introduce you to the members of the Baltimore League of Disenfranchised Thinkers." The head seemed proud of his association with this elite core of the intelligentsia. "This is Nathaniel Heller. Nathaniel is our resident nihilist."

Nathaniel stood up nonchalantly and offered his hand to Raymond in silence.

"Pleased to meet you, Nathaniel," said Raymond. Shaking Nathaniel's hand was like holding a piece of oily codfish. *Whew!*

Nathaniel was tall and thin and pale, with a narrow, elongated face that betrayed a severe acne problem in his youth. "And you are...a...?"

Raymond's eyes opened wide in reflexive terror. He felt a cool stream of adrenaline cascade down the backs of his legs. Raymond didn't like being asked that question. It was a downright invasion of privacy! "Ah...ah...I'm an apparitional causationist." Raymond swallowed hard. He felt as if he were driving an open convertible on a single-lane road high in the mountains, dodging falling rocks from the crumbling stone above as he negotiated hairpin precipice turns.

Henry Appletree continued on, "And this is Marcus Higgenbottom. Marcus is our resident stoic."

Marcus slowly stood up, snorted deeply, and put his large hands on his expansive hips. His perfectly round, bald head sat down between his massive shoulders like an anatomical afterthought. "I've never heard of apparitional causation, but I'm certainly open to your sharing this little-known worldview with us." He paused and pursed his lips. "I can handle anything you throw at me. That's my nature." He extended a meaty hand to Raymond.

"Pleased to meet you, Marcus." This handshake made Raymond wince. A power handshake, if ever there was one.

Henry smiled widely. He was pleased with the way things were progressing. "And this is Thomas Wolfbane. Tom is our resident Marxist."

Tom peeled himself out of his chair as if he were some kind of human slinky. "Welcome to our family, Ray." Tom was tall and wiry, with a short-cropped, gray beard meandering around a pointed chin. His face was tanned, giving evidence of either an outdoor labor job or membership in a local tanning salon. Tom extended his hand.

"Good to meet you, Tom." Ray shook Tom's hand and was somewhat surprised. Tom's shake actually seemed to be within normal limits.

"Well," said Henry, "let's make room for Raymond."

The four men, in unison, shifted here and there and everywhere with a flourish. Finally, order was restored and a chair was presented to Raymond, who dutifully took his place at one end of the two adjoined tables.

"Club soda and lime for Raymond," said Rick, gracefully placing Raymond's beverage before him. "And shall I keep the Dewar's coming for the rest of you gentlemen?"

The members of the Baltimore League of Disenfranchised Thinkers nodded in unison.

Henry leaned forward, his large head jutting out over the center of the table. Raymond was delighted to be situated as far as possible from the looming solipsist. He was also worried that Henry's chin might catch on fire. The flame from the candle beneath it was dangerously close.

"As president and spokesperson of our intellectual congregation," said Henry, "I want you to know how pleased we are to meet you, Ray—may I call you 'Ray'?—and how eager we are to hear your theory of apparitional causation." Henry slowly leaned backward, his head sliding and anchoring itself on the square, substantial muscles in the back of his neck. He sat quietly, staring at Ray with anticipation.

Ray cocked one eyebrow and glanced systematically around the table. Marcus, Tom, and Nathaniel were all riveted on him, their eyes wide open, and breathing heavily.

Ray furrowed his brow in concentration. "Uh…well, I guess I should give a brief summary of the theory." Ray felt himself stammering. "Uh…it is rather complex, you know."

The league nodded in unison, wide smiles appearing across their candlelit faces.

"The more complex the theory, the better," interjected Marcus. "I can withstand it. What doesn't kill my mind will strengthen it." He proudly looked at the other members of the League. "My mind is like a steel trap. Bring on your theory!"

Ray felt his face flush hot. He had the urge to run, screaming, from the Tusk Lounge. He no longer wanted to share the message with these insufferable dilettantes. But then, in a moment of composure that mysteriously overtook him, he reconsidered. *Sure,* he thought, *why not? Let's give the message a whirl. After all, it may not have been revealed to anyone other than myself.*

Rick, the ever-attentive bartender, delivered to the table the Dewar's in Italesse crystal glasses. Henry, Tom, Marcus, and Nathaniel reached for and oddly groped their respective rounded vessels before taking a sip en masse. Then, licking their lips spasmodically, they returned their attention to Raymond.

Raymond cleared his throat and began the maiden voyage of his holy message. "A few months ago, I had a series of dreams. And in those dreams, a message from beyond was communicated to me. During the communication, my mind acted like an electronic receiver. And once the message was delivered, and I had fully assimilated it and reflected upon its magnitude, I came to the only conclusion possible: the communicator of the message was none other than God."

Henry smiled and nodded knowingly. "And God is none other than yourself."

At this remark, Nathaniel choked on his scotch. After much guttural hacking and general respiratory distress, he finally settled down and spoke. "Ray, your conclusion that God spoke to you is completely irrational. God is...well, God is something the weak of heart have invented to give themselves the illusion of security." Nathaniel smirked and nodded his head dismissively. "Forget about it!"

Marcus raised his bushy eyebrows. "I wouldn't be so quick to judge. Ray did not desire this message to come to him. It came by its own necessity. I say we should hear him out!"

Tom, gazing into his scotch glass, shrugged his shoulders. "I will have to wait until the content of the conversation becomes earthbound before any comments I have will be germane." He looked up with a glimmer of hope in his eyes. "Please continue."

Ray sipped his club soda. Its effervescence tickled the membrane of his nostrils. He wrinkled his nose and continued. "Our modern science tells us that there are about one hundred chemical elements that make up the phenomenal world. And all of these elements are derived from hydrogen. By the process of transformational causation, or one thing or event transforming into another, the evolutionary scheme unfolds. Hydrogen transforms into helium; helium transforms into carbon; carbon transforms into oxygen; oxygen transforms into neon; neon transforms into magnesium. On and on it goes. The problem arises when we ask: where does the hydrogen come from?"

Henry, Nathaniel, Marcus, and Tom were sitting in various postures of concentration. Before, they were breathing heavily. Now, hardly breathing at all.

"We know that all of life is nothing other than energy. And we know that all energy—gravitational, kinetic, radiational, electrical, and magnetic—comes from the sun. But now I ask you: where does the sun get its energy? All the different forms of energy move transformationally. They do a dance, transforming one into another. Gravitational energy transforms into kinetic energy; kinetic energy transforms into radiation; radiation transforms into electricity; electricity transforms into magnetism. But now I ask you: where does gravity come from?"

Henry's large head was enjoying the exposition thus far; Marcus had saucers for eyes, but was withstanding the onslaught of information as well; Tom displayed infinite patience, waiting for the conversation to fall to earth from the stratosphere of the astronomers; Nathaniel, rolling his eyes with regularity, mumbled under his breath, "No fuckin' rhyme or reason to any of it."

"So our situation is this: all the chemical elements except for hydrogen come from hydrogen by the process of transformational causation; and all forms of energy except for gravity come from gravity by the process of transformational causation. But hydrogen and gravity cannot be gotten to by transformational causation. We can get to hydrogen and gravity only by some other pathway—and that pathway cannot be within the phenomenal world."

Marcus placed his scotch glass firmly on the table. "We are dealing with the problem of the *first cause.*"

"Precisely," answered Raymond.

"Look deep into your own mind for the answer!" said Henry.

"Look anywhere you like," growled Nathaniel, "there's no rhyme or reason to any of it!"

Tom leaned back in his chair. A thoughtful repose illuminated his tanned face. "Dialectically speaking, this is heading in a quite interesting direction."

"You say Ray's talk is giving you an erection?" interjected Nathaniel.

Henry's big head leaned forward over the table. "We'll have none of that, Nathaniel!"

Nathaniel shrugged complacently. "I'm sorry, Tom."

Tom nodded with acceptance. "No problem, Nate. I know where you're coming from."

Raymond, feeling the message urgently surging through him, continued: "So we see that the real origin of our universe is not to be found within space and time. Hence, it must lie beyond. And what is beyond space and time? The unchanging. The infinite."

Raymond stared at the glasses of scotch sitting on the table. The yellow-caramel color of the nectar shimmered in the elegant glassware like unpolished gold. Enticing, yes! But Ray was vigilant. He took a sip of club soda and continued: "A palpable paradox exists when we look for the first cause. We are genetically programmed to experience everything within the space-time continuum, and yet the first cause is beyond space and time. What are we to do?"

Henry smiled and slammed a meaty hand on the table. "This is not a paradox for me! No, sir! The origin of the universe is my own mind! My mind is the first cause!"

Nathaniel smirked and rubbed his hands over his face with exasperation. "None of it amounts to a hill of beans. We're born, we live, we die."

Marcus tossed back the remainder of his scotch. "Within space and time, beyond space and time—pay it no mind! Deal with it!"

Tom yawned, somewhat bored. "I understand life based on the dialectics of nature as characterized by Engels. When you step beyond space and time, I'm lost!"

Raymond felt a surge of compassion. "Let's see if we can't shed some light on this seemingly impenetrable conundrum." Ray paused in a moment of self-awareness. He was executing his destiny. Casting his God-sent message out into the cosmos. He concentrated his attention. "My message is this: From the very beginning, our knowledge has been based on a perceptual mistake. And everything that follows from that perceptual mistake is in error. Allow me to explain: Imagine that it is late at night and you are ready to retire. You open your bedroom door and flick on the light switch located on the wall just inside the door. But no light comes on. The light bulb has burned out. You peer into the bedroom using what shadowy illumination has cast itself from the light in the hallway. And, lo, you recoil. You see a long, dark snake stretched out in the middle of the floor. Your heart quickens and your mind begins to race. You quickly close the door and retreat to the living room. There you ponder, with anxiety, the different options for dealing with the unwanted visitor in your bedroom. Finally, you resolve not to deal with the dilemma until morning. You tell yourself that in the morning you will be refreshed and more at ease. For the time being, you decide to stuff some towels beneath the door of your bedroom to trap the snake inside, and, upon doing so, retire to your study and fall asleep on the couch. As you may expect, your sleep is fitful. The snake weighs heavily on your mind, making your sleep patterns tumultuous. Finally, you drift off into some gray, cavernous place where you hear your own breathing echoing in your ears like muffled voices speaking an unrecognizable language."

Henry, Marcus, Tom, and Nate leaned forward over the table, their collective intelligence reaching out for more of whatever it was Ray sought to convey to them.

Raymond's enthusiasm responded commensurately to their rapt attention. He felt like a stage actor vocalizing the truths of a transcendentally ingenious playwright. "Finally, you surface from your disenchanted slumber and see bright sunlight streaming through the window of your study. For a moment, your mind flounders about, trying to right itself, trying to remember what it doesn't want to remember. And then you do remember: *the snake!* You leap up from the couch and, with much trepidation, head for the pantry. You grab a long-handled broom from the cupboard and head for the bedroom. You pull away the towels from beneath the bedroom door and, with broom securely in hand, slowly push open the door. The first thing you notice is the bright sunshine flooding the room like a harbinger of some uncanny wisdom. And then you see it.

Stretched out on the middle of the floor. Your chest heaves and you drop the broom with welcome lightness in your heart. You see that the snake is none other than your own brown belt." Raymond breathed deeply. His throat was unpleasantly dry. He quickly took a hearty swallow of his club soda. "You see, my friends, when one thing is mistaken for another, the perception is the result of apparitional causation. We mistake appearance for reality. If you mistake a belt for a snake, nothing happens to the belt, but all of our thinking and behavior is dramatically affected because we think we're dealing with a snake. And this is precisely what has happened with the world that we live in." Raymond's face began to turn red. His voice became loud. "The first cause is apparitional! It is an appearance! The world that we nonchalantly take to be real is not real at all! The real is there, just like the belt is there, but we don't see it! The world we engage in is no more than a ghostly veil, and we cannot find the reality that lies behind it. We cannot see what is truly real as long as we believe in the apparition. And why, you ask, can we not get beyond the illusion of the apparition? Because we are genetically programmed to act in accordance with transformational causation which is, in fact, the illusion perpetrated by apparitional causation." Raymond was teetering on the edge of his chair. He thought his head would explode. "The problem is that we are programmed to run toward the illusion of the world of transformational causation. We are programmed to believe that the solution to all of our problems lies in action, in doing things that will bring about change or transformation." Raymond slumped forward, shook his head, and began to weep. He blubbered, "What we fail to grasp is this: We cannot find true happiness in a world of illusion because only what is real will make us completely happy. And the real is not subject to change. Action will not lead us to the real! The only way out of the impasse is to cheat the genetic programming." Raymond theatrically raised up both of his hands toward the heavens. "And, pray tell, how is that to be done? First, by some decreed messenger like myself, the truth of apparitional causation must be told. Then, we need to defy the genetic programming while still living in the world of illusion. We need to live in such a way as to not get caught in the web of transformational causation. We need to live in such a way as to no longer see action as the solution to all of our problems."

The room echoed a painful silence. With this last pronouncement, Raymond slumped down over the table, breathing hard, his bloodshot eyes staring straight ahead, focusing on nothing. Then he whispered, "Somehow, we must live in such a way that we always experience stillness. We must always remain inwardly still. It is in inner stillness that we experience the changeless, which is none other than reality itself."

Tom Wolfbane leaned forward with compassion. "Like it or not, the world we live in is a dialectical movement of matter. Change, or transformation as you call it, is essential. I'm afraid the genes cannot be cheated. And why would we want to cheat them in the first place?"

Raymond, still breathing hard, looked up halfheartedly. It was clear he had missed the mark with Tom. He spoke slowly in a whisper, enunciating every syllable. "We have to cheat the genes. We have to remain internally still in the midst of the dialectical movement. That stillness grounds us in the origin. It grounds us in the source. It is the grounding that brings lasting happiness."

Marcus Higgenbottom wiped his robust lips with the back of his hand. "Epictetus once said, 'Man is disturbed not by things, but by the views he takes of them.'" Marcus touched Ray gently on the shoulder. "I think you need to lighten up. Have a scotch. It'll make things seem much more palatable."

Nathaniel Heller raised his eyebrows and shook his head. "In this life no truth and no action is preferable to any other. I agree with Marcus. Have a jolt of scotch."

Henry Applegate ran his meaty hand across his expansive forehead and professorially cleared his throat. "Ray, all that you believe is true. And all that we, longtime members of the Baltimore League of Disenfranchised Thinkers, believe is true. For nothing exists outside of our own minds." Henry chortled and wrinkled his flat nose. "Let me amend that, and I do not mean any disrespect to my colleagues, but if the truth be known, there is nothing outside of *my* own mind."

Raymond, almost totally oblivious to his surroundings, suddenly spoke in a raspy whisper. "The thing is, I don't know how to cheat the genes. There must be some technique that one must commit oneself to. But damn if I know what it is."

Ten minutes later, Raymond stood alone in the back parking lot of the Brass Elephant. The cold dark of the late December night was creeping its way under Raymond's skin like icy tentacles. He contemplated the heavens as Immanuel Kant had done more than two centuries earlier. *Why, oh, why,* he thought, *in this already complex and difficult world, would God, or whoever is behind it all, genetically program the inhabitants of this planet to run after a self-defeating illusion? What kind of insidious cruelty is afoot? Or is it a case where an encounter with what is real would vanquish us?*

Chapter 40

Maddy Kerr sipped Aaron's homemade moonshine and felt the smooth bourbon go all the way down. She felt warm and safe sitting next to Aaron on his black leather couch, relaxing by the glowing fire in his cozy living room. She liked Aaron. There was something easy about him. She felt as if she could be herself with him.

Aaron gently stroked his graying beard. "You have a faraway look about you. What are you thinkin' about?"

Maddy smiled, self-satisfied. "I'm just happy to be here with you, Aaron. It's as simple as that."

Aaron nodded. "Okay. I can live with that."

Maddy laughed and tilted her head to the side. "Life takes some strange turns, doesn't it? How long have I known you? Probably thirty years? We were always civil to one another. Friendly acquaintances. But neither of us ever felt the need to reach out." Maddy shrugged happily, appreciating the irony. "Who would have ever thought I'd be sitting here with you on New Year's Eve, drinking your homemade moonshine, waiting to bring in the new millennium?"

Aaron raised his bushy eyebrows. "Timin' is everything."

Maddy shook her head and smiled. She felt renewed in spirit. She had never felt this way before. "Let's talk about spirituality. Tell me how you got into it." Maddy chortled, "God knows you weren't into it when you were burning up those cars in high school."

Aaron shrugged good-naturedly. "You know, me bein' a mean son-of-a-bitch actually had a lot to do with it. After I did my time in juvenile prison, I knew I wasn't long for this earth if I didn't straighten myself out." Aaron took a pull of bourbon from his glass tumbler. "When I look back on it, it all makes sense. But while I was goin' through it, hell, I couldn't see no rhyme or reason to any of it."

Maddy squinted in concentration. "Tell me all about it. I'm really interested."

Aaron smiled and nodded. He felt a little embarrassed. "Are you sure you want to hear this? It gets pretty funky."

"Yeah. I'm sure."

Aaron flashed a look of consent and continued. "When I got out of juvenile prison, somethin' propelled me to just keep movin'. If I stayed in one spot for more than a day or two, I felt like my skin was on fire. And the only way I could cool down was to get out and keep movin'. I had about four hundred dollars to my name. I decided to drive to Eugene, Oregon. Don't know exactly why. But it was far away and seemed like a good idea. So I went cross-country in my little Ford Escort." Aaron paused and stared at Maddy. After some consideration, he held out his hands, palms up. "I don't rightly know why I'm gonna tell you what I'm gonna tell you. It's somethin' I've kept to myself for over thirty years."

Maddy sat quietly for a moment and then took a deep breath. "Aaron, do you want me to keep what you say to me in confidence?"

"Yeah. I do."

"Okay. Whatever you say stays here. You can trust me."

Aaron nodded. "I know I can. That's why I'm gonna tell you." He pursed his lips. "I got a confession to make. You know when you found *Zen Mind, Beginner's Mind* out back behind the Elk Head? Well, I put it there. I knew you needed it. That you were ready for it. How I knew, I can't tell you. But I knew." Aaron shrugged his massive shoulders. "You'll understand when I tell you my story."

Maddy blinked her big, brown eyes twice, as if she were testing the reality of the situation. "I don't know what to say."

"Don't say anything. I'll do the talkin' for now."

Chapter 41

Six bearded men with white cotton turbans wrapped around their heads huddled over a wooden table covered with a worn, ink-marked paper that had been rolled out and secured on its edges with chunks of busted-up mortar. The men wore loose-fitting, white cotton shirts, light brown cotton trousers, and sandals. The glare from three bare light bulbs, hanging from the ceiling in wire cages, illuminated the small, damp basement like anachronistic torches ablaze in an ancient, subterranean cave.

The men systematically pointed at various places on the paper. They nodded. They smiled. They embraced warmly. They rolled out thin mats of wool fabric. They dropped to their knees in prayer.

Chapter 42

"When I arrived in Eugene, it was mid July," said Aaron. "I was nineteen years old and had no idea what the hell I was doin'. But everybody was excited about the Oregon Country Fair, so I caught a ride with some students and went out to a wooded area off Highway 126. The fair was a hell of a good time. Part of it was like a surrealistic parade with people in bizarre animal outfits, chantin' and drummin' and singin' and dancin'. It was quite an eyeful. At any rate, I was sittin' under a big old oak tree havin' a beer when a tall, pasty-skinned man with a shock of pure white hair appeared out of the woods and sat down next to me. He was probably sixty. Nice enough fella. Real polite and friendly. But he had the most peculiar eyes. They were bright blue. Crystal blue. And they looked like glass. They were real shiny and there wasn't any life in 'em. You could almost see your reflection in 'em. That shoulda told me somethin' right there. But what did I know? Anyhow, we're talkin' and he says to me, 'Son, I'll tell you where you gotta go. Mesa Verde. You gotta go to the ancient Indian cliff dwellin's.' I said, 'Where's Mesa Verde?' He said, 'Southwest Colorado.' I said, 'Shoot, that's back in the other direction. I just got here in Eugene.' He shook his head and said, 'That's where you gotta go.'"

Aaron leaned forward, picked up the jug of moonshine off the coffee table, and refreshed his and Maddy's glasses. "So the next mornin', I left for Mesa Verde. For some crazy reason, I had it in my mind that I had to drive straight through. I swear it felt like there was some invisible hand pushin' me to keep on drivin'. Anyway, by early evenin', I picked up Route 50 cuttin' across Nevada. I stayed on 50 right into Utah where 50 and Route 6 double up. By that time it was close to midnight." Aaron suddenly sat back and slowly shook his head. "That's when it happened." Aaron sat still as a statue. Hardly breathing.

"You all right?" asked Maddy, with genuine concern.

Aaron shrugged and laughed halfheartedly. "You know, it happened over thirty years ago. And I still get choked up when I think about it."

Maddy winced. She could feel his discomfort. "What happened, Aaron?"

Aaron temporarily diverted himself from the emotion of the memory. "You mind if I light up a cigar?"

Maddy nodded. "Get your cigar."

"You want one?"

Maddy smiled gently. "No, thanks."

Aaron got up, crossed the room, and selected a Nat Sherman Hamilton cigar from his homemade, cedar humidor. He grabbed a cutter and Zippo lighter from the table drawer beneath the humidor and returned to the couch. In a mood of quiet reflection, he clipped his cigar and fired it up, carefully assuring that it was well lit. He took a hefty draw and blew a blue-gray swirl of smoke up to the log rafters ten feet above him. Leaning back, he nodded at Maddy. "It was on Route 6, on the vast, open Utah plain, that I disappeared." Aaron pursed his lips. "I fuckin' disappeared."

Maddy quizzically cocked her head. "What do you mean, 'disappeared'?"

Aaron nodded. "I disappeared. For about five hours." Aaron gazed at his cigar, cradling it gently in his fingers like a delicate china doll. "It was midnight, and I was in the blackest dark you can imagine, drivin' fast on Route 6. Nobody was out on the plain but me. And then, I saw flashes of bright, white light in my rearview mirror. I slowed down and studied 'em. There were two orbs of light hangin' low in the sky. They were probably twenty-five feet apart, and about a hundred yards behind me. As I drove, the lights seemed to be followin' me at a steady distance. So, I did some experimentin'. I'd speed up, and the lights would speed up. I'd slow down, and the lights would slow down."

Maddy looked at him, perplexed. "What the hell were they?"

"Believe me, that's the fuckin' question I was askin' myself."

Maddy took a deep breath. "I don't like where this is going."

"Well, all of a sudden, the lights were on top of me. They were straight above me." Aaron shook his head in silence. "And that's when I disappeared."

Maddy exhaled demonstratively and belted back her bourbon.

"The next thing I knew, the sun was comin' up, and I was sittin' in my car at the bottom of Mesa Verde. I have no memory at all of how I got from the Utah plain to Southwest Colorado."

Maddy leaned toward him. "I don't follow you."

Aaron shook his head. "I can only tell you what happened. I can't explain it."

"All right. Tell me what happened."

"Like I said, I disappeared. I went somewhere, but I don't know where. And when I came back, I was different. I mean, *completely* different. My face and body were the same, but inside I was completely different. My mind was completely different. I didn't recognize my own thoughts. To this day, I don't recognize my own thoughts. Why they are what they are and where they come from are mysteries to me."

Maddy shook her head, puzzled.

"And I have exceptional powers."

Maddy blinked hard. "Powers?"

"Yeah. I have powers. I'm some kind of shaman or mystic. I know things that I shouldn't know, and I do things that I shouldn't be able to do. Hell, Maddy, I can bring dead creatures back to life. I can heal the sick. I can see straight into the heart of good and evil."

Maddy sat still, mouth agape. "I don't know what to say."

"There ain't nothin' to say. I'm as baffled as you are." Aaron sat quietly, listening to his own thoughts. "I think I was abducted by aliens. I think the guy I met in Eugene, the one with the glass eyes—I think he was all part of the plan. He got me out there on the open plain where he knew the aliens would be waitin' for me. It's the only conclusion I can come up with. And those aliens did somethin' to me. They surely did."

"Jesus, Aaron. This is really fucked up."

"You don't need to be afraid of me, Maddy. I'm non-violent. I used to be a violent motherfucker, but not anymore. And I'm not insane. I'm as clear and forthright as one can be."

Maddy looked at Aaron. Considered his warm, honest face. "I believe you. I do."

Outside the cabin, snow was gently falling in the dark silence, falling as if orchestrated by some cosmic algorithm suggesting an intelligence behind the chaos of the world.

Maddy felt the need to change the subject, if only for a little while. "So you took a look at me over at the Elk Head, sized me up, and saw that I was aching for spiritual growth?"

Aaron smiled innocently. "More or less."

"Why *Zen Mind, Beginner's Mind?* Why not…why not the Bible?"

"I gave you the book you need. Trust me." Aaron puffed contemplatively on his cigar. "That's the book I read. The only one."

"The *only* one? What's that mean?"

"That's what they told me to read. That one book. They said it's the only one I'll ever need to read."

Maddy crinkled her comely, freckled nose. "*Who* told you?"

"The aliens. That directive was clearly engraved in my mind when I came back to the earthly realm." Aaron nodded demonstratively. "They're right, Maddy. Live the Zen life with complete devotion, and you'll be all right."

"And that's why you meditate over at Thich Nhat Hanh's place?"

"Yeah. It all seems to fit."

Maddy sat still, lost in thought. "You think Shunryu Suzuki was an alien?"

Aaron winked mischievously. "I've thought about that. And my answer is no. I think the aliens directed me to a livin' saint right here on earth. I think they know that we need a human example to guide our lives by."

"Do you think all aliens are benevolent like the ones you encountered?"

"Nope. Don't think so."

"Why do you say that?"

"It's not that hard to figure. Life, no matter where you find it, involves a clash of opposites. Without opposin' forces, the world would not move. It wouldn't function. That's the way it's been set up. Without opposition, there would be no evolution. Good and evil are just a given. We have to learn to endure the battle."

Maddy slowly nodded. She was taking her time digesting Aaron's insights. "I've got another question. Did you ever get to the cliff dwellings at Mesa Verde?"

"Oh, yeah. I sure did."

"What happened?"

"Nothin' much from an external point of view. But internally, I felt like I'd come home. I sat down in one of the caves and rubbed my hands along the dirt floor and knew that I had lived there a long time ago. Somethin' inside me connected with that cave." Aaron smiled and puffed on his cigar. "It wasn't really me that connected. It was the alien intelligence that was livin' in me. That's what connected. That's what lived there before."

"Are you saying that aliens at one time resided in the cliff dwellings?"

"Yeah. I think so. That's why the glass-eyed man sent me there. To rekindle that alien spark within me. Bein' home and really feelin' it can empower you." Aaron sat quietly with his thoughts. "That kind of empowerment gives you an anchor. With that anchor, you can withstand whatever shitstorm life throws at you."

Maddy rolled her eyes good-naturedly and sipped her bourbon. "I'm not going to argue with you." She looked at her watch: 12:20 a.m. She smiled and put her arm around Aaron. "Happy New Year, my dear friend."

Aaron smiled and leaned into Maddy. "And to you."

Aaron then turned inward and saw it. Flashing across the screen of his consciousness. Ghostly presences of destruction and mass insanity.

Aaron looked at Maddy intently. "Read the book. You'll need it more than ever."

Maddy laid her head on Aaron's massive chest. "All right. I will."

Chapter 43

January 10, 2001

Dear Alex,

Gosh. I don't know what to say. Your last letter is one for the ages. You're living in a cave? With Hindu and Buddhist monks? Traversing the ocean of madness (your words, not mine)? Sorry I can't be of more help—but in this journey, you're on your own.

As for me, I've learned something. I'm my own worst enemy. My own insufferable hubris is what keeps my self-loathing alive. To make a long story short, I made a presentation to the Baltimore League of Disenfranchised Thinkers. I introduced the theory (which I deem extremely significant) of apparitional causation. Whew! That was a mistake that bears no repetition. Talk about a disenfranchised theory! Anyway, I'll no longer be pontificating to that odd group of cerebral misfits.

The long and the short of it is this: I know what I know (my theory, that is), and that's just fine with me. Mum's the word from here on out. I'm just going to live a simple life and follow the dictates of my conscience.

Oh, and I've stopped drinking. The booze just doesn't mix well with my DNA. Finally figured that one out!

So, dear brother, I bid you good blessings.
Ray

Chapter 44

Walt Dropo paced the dingy gray linoleum floor, hands shoved down deep into his pockets, body hunched over as if he were bearing some heavy, unforgiving weight.

"What time's he supposed to get here?" asked Deputy Ned Neville.

Walt frowned at Ned as if he were an unwarranted nuisance and glanced at his watch: 3:15 p.m. "Fifteen minutes ago," he answered. Walt walked to the window and looked out onto Jefferson Street. The moment he saw the squad car, his heart kicked into arrhythmia. He felt dizzy and saw sparkling silver stars dance across his field of vision. "He's here," the sheriff said in a gravelly murmur.

"Say what?"

"*He's here!*" Walt yelled.

"Well, shit, Walt, don't take it out on me!"

The door to the sheriff's office swung open. The prisoner, with his head down, came in first. He was tall and lanky, with an abnormally small, round head and buzz-cut, black hair that looked as if it were painted on his skull. His right arm was lassoed to his body with a leather strap, and his legs were in ankle chains. He had no left arm. The tattered left sleeve of his soiled, black T-shirt hung like a dark shadow enshrouding a noumenal phantom of doom.

Matt Lawlor followed the prisoner, pushing him along with his left hand. His right hand held a black billy club at the ready.

Walt stood with his back to the window, his heart pounding erratically beneath his breastbone. "Hey, Sheriff Lawlor. So this is the prisoner?"

Matt looked up and smirked. "Looks like it, don't it?"

"Yeah. Take him to the cell in the back. Deputy Neville will show you where."

Neville, the prisoner, and Lawlor passed through the front office like misfits in a seedy traveling circus. Walt, not knowing what to do, just stood there. A man lost to himself. *Gotta kick myself into gear*, he thought. *Gotta fuckin' deal with this!*

Lawlor walked back into the office, expertly flipping his billy club with his right hand. He was chewing a big wad of pink bubblegum. "Well, Walt, he's all yours now."

Walt nodded, none too pleased.

"Let me give you a word of advice. Don't take the leg irons off. And always keep a row of bars between you and him."

Suddenly, Ned Neville rushed into the office. He was breathing hard and had an oozing clump of foul, gray spittle lodged on the torso of his dark green cardigan sweater. "Motherfucker spit on me! Son-of-a-bitch!"

"You're lucky that's all he's done," said Lawlor complacently. "At my place, he damn near bit off Jerry Spicer's finger. Took eight stitches to close it."

Ned looked as if he was going to cry. Walt shook his head with a hearty mixture of fear and disgust. "Go clean yourself off, Ned. Go on now."

Ned, his head hanging down with embarrassment, scurried for the bathroom.

Lawlor stopped swinging the billy club. He squinted. "Seriously, Walt, this guy is a real bad-ass. Be careful."

Walt nodded, very unsure of himself.

"You got those papers I faxed to you?"

"Yeah." Walt went to his desk and grabbed a folder full of loose papers.

"You gotta sign my prisoner release."

"Yeah." Walt found the forms, signed them in duplicate, and handed one to Lawlor.

Ned walked back into the office, sullen and withdrawn. "I'm gonna go on patrol." He grabbed his coat off the coatrack and quickly darted through the door.

Matt Lawlor wrinkled his red, bulbous nose and snorted. "Step outside with me, Walt."

Walt threw on his leather jacket and joined Matt out on the sidewalk. Matt chucked his bubblegum into the street, unzipped his bulky, police-issued ski jacket and pulled a pack of Camels from the breast pocket of his shirt. "Want a cigarette?"

Walt shook his head.

Matt lit up with a sleek, silver Zippo lighter and took a deep draw off the unfiltered cigarette. He looked up and stared out into the vastness of the gray winter sky. "I want to talk to you off the record, Walt. Can I do that?"

Walt nodded. He was cold and filled with fear of what waited for him inside.

"There's somethin' seriously wrong with that prisoner. You'll find out what I mean soon enough."

Walt nodded. His head felt like a lead weight.

"You know, drivin' up here today, I had a notion to kill him. That's what I really wanted to do. I thought I'd make it look like he was tryin' to escape, and then I'd pop him one." Matt gritted his teeth and spat on the sidewalk. "But I didn't do it."

Walt kicked at the sidewalk, absentmindedly. He wanted to disappear.

"What I'm sayin' is, if somethin' were to happen to him, I wouldn't hold it against you. Nobody in their right mind would."

Walt pulled the collar of his jacket snug around his neck.

"You get my drift?"

"Yeah."

"I'm just sayin' that the world would be a better place without his kind."

"Yeah."

Matt Lawlor reached down and adjusted his crotch. He inhaled a final draw off the Camel and flicked the lit butt into the street's slushy muck. "I'm outta here." He turned to Walt and nodded, communicating silently.

Walt nodded. "Yeah."

Matt hopped into his squad car and drove off. Walt stood outside the sheriff's office in frozen deportment, as if he were a cigar store Indian that had been positioned there long ago and then forgotten. The sun was starting to disappear behind the blue-gray mountains to the west, and the temperature was dropping fast. Walt wondered about the prisoner. *How could he stand this fuckin' cold, wearin' nothin' but a T-shirt?*

Chapter 45

Alice Thornberry cleaned her soup bowl in the kitchen sink, placed it in the plastic dish drainer, and then shuffled over to the kitchen cupboard for her bottle of I.W. Harper. She held the bottle in her hand and eyed the label with sustained satisfaction. It was her nectar of the gods. She shambled over to the kitchen table in double anticipation. As the bottle thudded down next to the latest edition of the *Valley News*, Alice pulled a handful of Vermont Powerball lottery tickets out of her overalls pocket. She spread them out on the table, returned to the cupboard for a shot glass, and then settled down before her two favorite treats. She deftly unscrewed the cap on the bottle of I.W. Harper, her practiced fingers belying their adversity, and poured herself a shot. As she took it down, her eyes closed gently while the warm libation cascaded into her belly and gradually seeped through the synapses of her seventy-two-year-old brain. A grateful smile and appreciative nod closed the introductory ritual, and, lottery hopes beckoning, Alice opened the newspaper to the winning Powerball number and began comparing it to her tickets.

When she got to the third ticket, she stopped and cocked her head. She carefully glanced back and forth at the Match 5 number on her ticket and the one in the paper. "Son-of-a-bitch," she mumbled. She leaned back and rubbed her eyes with the palms of her wrinkled hands. Doubting her eyesight and good fortune, she compared the digits once more before conceding to well-founded excitement. "Well, lookee here! Lookee here! We got ourselves a winner!" Alice shouted. Feeling a stinging stream of adrenaline surge through her chest, she looked back down at the paper and checked her winnings. "Lookee here! Two hundred thousand dollars!" At this point, Alice began shaking in her chair. She felt as if she were a spinning top. A wail of laughter came roaring out of her like some incongruous banshee yell. She laughed and laughed, and then the laughter quickly turned into a coughing frenzy. She coughed and coughed, reaching for the I.W. Harper, struggling to catch her breath.

Chapter 46

To recognize that the world arises through apparitional causation is to understand that the world we experience is an illusion. What we experience is based on a mistake in perception. Believe me, if we saw the world correctly, we could find the first cause. We could find God as readily as we can find the fingers on our own hands. But we are genetically programmed to experience our world within space and time. And that's the apparatus for the illusion.

Who is the grand master of the illusion? God. That's as good a name as any. And why, you ask, would God do this to us? Why would God perpetrate such an illusion? Is it because God doesn't want to be found? Perhaps. Is it because he wants to remain mysterious? Possibly. Is it because he wants us to look for him in all the wrong places? Maybe. But why? So that we'll tire ourselves out and give up? Maybe. Perhaps that is the key to knowing God. By exhausting ourselves in our attempts to know him, we give up—and only then, in a state of complete receptivity, are we able to see him. Or is it a case where God doesn't reveal himself out of compassion for us? Perhaps our witnessing him would catastrophically destroy us. Hmmm. Lots of questions with no answers.

The rare few on whom this wisdom is bestowed know that if we got into the web of apparition by a mistake in perception, then we can get out of it only by undoing the apparition. And what, pray tell, would that entail? Nothing other than cheating the genes and going against the programming that God has set into motion. We need to live in the world without getting caught in the web of the illusion.

Raymond rolled in his sleep and woke with a start. He rubbed his tearing eyes. *That damn dream continues to haunt me,* he thought. *How do I cheat the genes? Who can tell me?*

Chapter 47

Walt Dropo sat hunched over the kitchen table, stirring his coffee. Across from him, in her stained, pink bathrobe, sat his wife of thirty years, Matilda Hughes Dropo. She was short and frumpy and wore a patch over her left eye. Lost the eye when she was four to a stray arrow shot by her older brother. Her skin was pasty pale, and the black patch looked like a dark, intrusive hole just right of center in her moribund face. Matilda liked watching reruns of *Hollywood Squares*. That was her favorite thing to do. Walt swallowed his coffee in quiet desperation. Then, out of the bitter morning silence of the Dropo household, the phone rang.

Matilda pushed herself away from the table and labored over to the black wall phone hanging next to the back door. She picked up the phone. "Hello? ...Yeah, he's here." Matilda let the phone hang down the wall on its curlicued cord and walked away. "For you, Walt."

Walt looked at his Timex. Seven in the morning. "Who is it?"

"Sue Warren."

"What she want?"

"To talk to you." Matilda yawned and meandered out of the kitchen, impassive and indifferent.

Walt got up, walked over to the wall by the back door, and reached down for the phone. "Hi, Sue. What can I do you for?"

Chapter 48

When Walt Dropo pulled up in front of Alice Thornberry's clapboard farmhouse, Sue Warren was waiting for him. She stood in the falling snow next to her salt-encrusted Subaru Forrester. A bulky, green parka enveloped her like a cocoon, and she was leaning on an old hiking stick that had a leather strap looped through a hole about six inches from the top. Sue was none too good with her balance. An inoperable brain tumor threw her equilibrium out of whack.

"Hey, Sue."

"Hey, Walt."

The two bystanders of life stared at each other uncomfortably. Finally, Walt spoke. "Tell me what happened."

Sue rubbed the back of her emaciated hand across her cracked, ice blue lips. A pointy stocking cap sat atop her bony forehead, and her gray, beady eyes looked as if they were frozen in their dark sockets, perhaps never to move again. "Me and Alice had a plan today. We was goin' into Rutland for the flea market. Wanted to get there early." Sue suddenly stopped speaking. Just stood there like a wax figure in some long-forgotten museum of the damned. And then, just as suddenly, she began speaking again. "Well, when I got here, she wouldn't answer the door. I thought that was mighty strange, Alice not answerin' the door.

So I walked around back and looked through the kitchen winder." Sue stopped again.

Walt nodded and waited. He figured this spasmodic way of talking was due to her tumor.

"When I looked through the winder, I saw her lyin' across the table. She wasn't movin'." Sue struggled to swallow, her throat dry from breathing through her mouth. "That's when I called ya." Sue's old, worn face contorted into a smile. She patted the big pocket of her parka. "Just got this here cell phone. It already came in handy."

Walt sighed and pursed his lips. "Okay, Sue. You go on home now. I'll take a look inside."

Sue nodded and climbed into the Subaru with assistance from her hiking stick. She started the engine and rolled down the window. She leaned her head out and nodded at Walt. "I think she's dead in there. That's what I think."

Walt slowly blinked his cold, tired eyes. "Why do you say that?"

"'Cause Alice wouldn't sleep on her kitchen table. She wouldn't do that."

Walt nodded and stuffed his cold hands deep into his pockets. Walking to the front porch, he turned back to stare at Sue's Subaru disappearing into the white of the winter storm. He looked at his Timex. Seven twenty. The snow-blanched landscape recaptured his gaze as thoughts bubbled up to the surface of his consciousness. *Cold. Snow. A psychotic killer with one arm wearin' nothin' but a T-shirt.*

The sheriff swallowed hard and tried the front door. Locked. He walked around back and stared through the kitchen window. It was just as Sue had described it. He tried the back door. Open! Entering the kitchen, he immediately held his nose. The heavy stench of death wafted through the room and clung to the walls like greasy tentacles. He leaned over Alice and studied what was before him.

Alice was slumped over the Formica table, her left arm folded under her, her left hand clutching the center of her chest. Her right arm was stretched out, her right hand grasping the bottle of I.W. Harper. Walt leaned down to examine the lottery tickets that were strewn across the table, and in so doing, saw the corner of a piece of paper protruding from Alice's left hand. He stepped back and straightened up, covered his mouth and took a deep breath. He stared at the corner of paper in Alice's hand for a long time. Lost in some contemplative reverie that was not of his own making, he pursed his lips and leaned forward, carefully prying the paper from Alice's final grasp. Another lottery ticket. Walt looked at the Match Five number, wrinkling his nose and blinking hard. The winning lottery number on the open page of the *Valley News* repeated itself on the ticket in his hand. He slowly backed away from the table. A strange and lilting melody filled his head, a melody he had never heard anywhere in this lifetime. He listened receptively, allowing what might be some ancient hymn of grace to fill his head with the mystery and wonder of the truly unexpected.

Chapter 49

Aaron Riley leaned his massive forearms on the icy railing of the Route 4 bridge high above the deep, narrow, rocky walls of the Quechee Gorge. He stared down at the nearly frozen Ottaquechee River, lodged like a brittle, gray skeleton in the jagged cleft 165 feet below. Casting his gaze northward, he beheld the same cold and dreary grayness stretching into the infinity of air and sky, and reflexively pulled over his head the hood of his warm, insulated parka. Aaron turned to his right and nodded at Maddy. She looked like some lost urchin, bundled up in her ski jacket and thick wool stocking cap. "Let's get some coffee."

Maddy nodded and stuffed her gloved hands into her jacket pockets.

The two cold wayfarers walked across the bridge, climbed into Aaron's Nissan Pathfinder, and drove a mile west on Route 4 to the Simon Pearce Restaurant at the Quechee Mill. They sat in the terraced, glass-enclosed café overlooking the majestic falls of the Ottaquechee River, drinking coffee and eating coarse Ballymaloe bread with sweet butter.

Aaron smiled beneath his bushy, graying beard. "The word *sadhana* means spiritual practice. It's through sadhana that we learn how to live in a way that's both sane and respectful. Unfortunately, it's damn near impossible to do."

Maddy sipped her coffee, looking perplexed. "Why is it so difficult to be sane and respectful? Doesn't it just make sense to live that way?"

Aaron smiled impishly. "If it's so damn easy, why are you sittin' here tryin' to learn from me?" He shook his head. "Look at this messed-up world and all the people in it. How many would you say are truly sane and respectful?"

Maddy sat in silence.

"Yep. You got it." Aaron sipped his coffee. "The problem is this: Before we can live in a sane and respectful way, we have to be linked to the truth of this life. If we don't really know what's goin' on here, we have no clue about how to be sane and respectful." Aaron looked out on the rapid falls of the river. "See all the commotion in the falls? All the incessant movement and force and energy? That's all superficial. And if you live life that way, you'll be superficial. You'll be causin' one hell of a commotion, but your life won't have any substance to it. That's the thing about sanity and respect. They have a substance to 'em that runs deep and still. It's a tricky situation. For some reason, we're genetically programmed to live in ways that are not sane and respectful. And that programmin' glues us to the superficial. Sadhana is about extricatin' yourself from that gluey mess." Aaron looked at Maddy and smiled gently. "You need to wipe some butter from your mouth."

Maddy laughed self-consciously and wiped her mouth with the back of her hand. "Did I get it?"

Aaron nodded. "You got it." He turned and looked at the falls. "We need to live in the midst of the spray of the falls, and yet remain dry and comfortable. We have to learn to discriminate between the real and the unreal, the substance and the superficial."

Maddy leaned back in her chair attentively. "How did you learn this?"

"I didn't learn it. Not in any conventional way. The aliens infused me with this wisdom. I'm just lucky they chose me to be their instrument."

"I guess I'm lucky as well."

"I hope so." Aaron looked out into the pallid cast of the bitter cold January morning. "There are three equations of truth in this life. Love is truth. Freedom is truth. Peace is truth. Love, freedom, and peace are the pure substances beneath the constantly blowin' winds of superficiality. These are the substances that you want to catch hold of. The problem is that you're genetically programmed to catch hold of 'em in biological ways." Aaron smiled patiently. "The pure substances, however, are not biological. They're spiritual. In sadhana, we try to catch hold of the pure substances, minimizin' the biological necessities as much as possible."

Maddy's head was swimming in a sea of looming confusion. "So, let me try this out. We seek love in a biological way. We seek it in...sex."

"Yup. But sex, in and of itself, isn't love. In fact, it has little to do with it."

"I see the problem." Maddy contemplated her next statement. "And we seek freedom in a biological way. We seek it in...the avoidance of death. We occupy ourselves obsessively with money and fancy possessions in order to avoid the biologically inevitable."

"Right. We think that if we're rich and can buy whatever we want, we can be free. But it ain't so."

"And we seek peace in a biological way. We seek it in...complete satiation."

"Precisely. And yet, satiation is momentary at best. Soon, we think of somethin' else that we want, and we're restless again. So we see that biological solutions to catchin' hold of love, freedom, and peace are not solutions at all. At best, they're superficial, momentary substitutes."

Maddy smirked. "We're fucked."

Aaron nodded. "Pretty much so." He sipped the last of his coffee. "Let's drive over to the Harpoon Brewery and have a beer."

Maddy shook her head and laughed out loud. "Let's see. Coffee and beer. Sounds like you're leaning toward the fulfillment of biological necessities."

Aaron smiled and shrugged. *What, me worry?*

Chapter 50

Walt Dropo sat in the Halfmoon Police squad car on an abandoned parking lot at the corner of Jefferson and Palmer Streets. He sat behind a concrete block building that used to be a Sunoco filling station. Nothing was left but the worn block shell and a rusted-out water tank. It was two in the afternoon, but to Walt it was as if time had stopped and a loneliness which knew no hour had claimed him as a child of the damned. He leaned up against the driver's side window and looked up at the sky, but it seemed as if there were no sky. Just gray clouds hovering heavily, negating any sky that might have once been there.

The sheriff reached over to the passenger's seat, grabbed another can of Budweiser, and popped the top. *Five down, one to go,* he thought, taking a heavy draw off the brain fogger. Aware of his heart thudding steadily against his breastbone, Walt thought about the one-armed prisoner sitting in that cold cell a mere three blocks away. He thought about what he would say to him and how he'd respond to whatever the prisoner might say back. But the timid lawman didn't get far with his thoughts. He really couldn't as long as the fear persisted. The can of Bud in his grasp focused Walt's stare and his hope that it might be the one to put him over the edge. Over the edge where fear is forgotten, if only for a little while. If only for a little while.

Chapter 51

Aaron Riley turned onto Route 5 off I-91. Maddy sat next to him, happily lost in the absence of thought. The two of them were settling into each other. They really didn't speak much. They just eased into each other's congenial presence with genuine contentment. About a mile down Route 5, Aaron turned left into the Harpoon Brewery. It was a little after two in the afternoon and the parking lot was empty save for a couple of employees' trucks parked off to one side. Aaron pulled up to the front of the microbrewery and shut off the engine. He and Maddy hopped out of the Pathfinder and stood in the parking lot, looking up at the sky. The dense gray canopy above them began to swirl and dissipate as if by magic—as if it were being erased by some supernatural process that only the gods could fathom.

Aaron squinted at the eddying, disappearing cloud cover. "Never seen anything like this. Strange."

"Yeah. Very strange."

"It's like some kind of sign."

"It is? Why do you say that?"

"It's just a feelin' I got." Aaron looked down at the snow-covered ground as if he were searching for something lost. Then he looked back up at the tumultuous, reeling sky of light and dark. "Somethin's gonna happen. I don't know what it is. But it's gonna happen. And it probably ain't gonna be good."

"You're frightening me," said Maddy.

Aaron shrugged. "Nothin' to be scared of. What's gonna happen is gonna happen. Nobody in this world can stop the inevitable."

Maddy shivered in the raw cold of the afternoon. "Let's go in."

Aaron smiled. "Yeah. Let's get ourselves a beer."

When they opened the door to the front entrance of the brewery, they were hit by a wall of overwhelming olfactory sweetness. Aaron unzipped his parka and inhaled deeply. "Ah. I love the smell of yeast. Kinda makes your eyes tingle."

Maddy shook her head in delight. She really liked Aaron. There was no subterfuge with him. And he displayed a kindness that made her feel open to be herself. "What should we order?" asked Maddy, as they approached the bar.

"I'm gettin' a pint of the UFO Hefeweizen. It's an unfiltered wheat beer. I think you'd like it."

Maddy nodded at the barkeep. She tilted her head toward Aaron. "I'll have what he's having."

The barkeep nodded back. He was young and bearded and didn't seem to have a care in the world. "I'm Joe. Welcome to the Brewery. If you want to take a tour of the facilities, have at it. And if you've got questions, I'll be happy to answer them."

Aaron nodded and smiled. "Okay, Joe. Thanks much."

Joe pulled two pints of the Hefeweizen into frosted glasses, stuck a small wedge of lemon on each rim, and placed them in front of Aaron and Maddy. "Should I start a tab?"

"Yeah. I think we'll be here for a while." Aaron studied his beer, holding the glass up to the light. "See how cloudy the golden color is? That's because the yeast has remained unfiltered." He took a long, slow draw and gently smacked his lips. "Now that's a beer for the ages."

Maddy tried hers and nodded. "It has a citrus flavor."

"Yeah. The yeast does that. And of course the lemon doesn't hurt."

Joe smiled and looked at Maddy. "I don't think you'll be asking me any questions. Your companion seems to be very well versed in the beer trade."

Maddy shrugged. "He's just a show-off!"

Aaron kicked Maddy's boot. *Thud!* "Watch your tongue, now."

Maddy nodded and smiled. "Okay. I'll be good."

"I'll leave you to your own devices," said Joe. "I've got some paperwork to catch up on. I'll be right over there behind the merchandise counter. Holler if you need me."

"Okay, Joe. Will do." Aaron sipped his beer and lowered his eyebrows in concentration. "Let's pick up where we left off at

Simon Pearce's." He nodded to himself and sat in silence, inwardly perceiving some nuance of wisdom. "A gene pool will only survive if it drives itself toward the fulfillment of biological necessities. And we're only kiddin' ourselves if we think we can overcome the hard-wirin'. But we've seen the futility of experiencin' the true nature of love, freedom, and peace when we're attendin' to biological necessities. The best we can do is to weaken our attachment to the biological necessities as much as possible. We should attend to 'em, but not obsess over 'em; attend to 'em, but not complicate 'em." Aaron chuckled and shrugged his massive shoulders. *How strange this life is,* he thought. *A big lug like me bein' the carrier of such wisdom.* He smiled happily and continued: "The bottom line is this: we need to live a simple, uncomplicated, unselfish life. If we can forget ourselves in the livin', we can just be. And by allowin' ourselves to be, we allow everything to be. And that's when love, freedom, and peace will fill your heart. Love, freedom, and peace are not biological experiences—they're spiritual ones."

Maddy wrinkled her freckled nose. "Keep talking. If you keep going, I think I'll get it."

"All right. I'll keep goin'." Aaron paused and closed his eyes. Then he opened them and nodded. "Our body is not separate from the environment. It *is* the environment. If we allow our body to move rhythmically with nature, and not allow our ego to get involved, the biological necessities of the body will not become complicated. Eatin' will take place only when we're hungry and only for the simple act of nourishment. Eatin' that focuses on gratifyin' the ego separates you from the food. But the fact is you *are* the food." Aaron sipped his beer with great concentration. "The moment I swallow, I *am* the beer." He winked and smiled. "We should sleep when we're tired. We should take naps. We should just curl up and let go. Sleepin' out of routine or habit or laziness or avoidance of life is ego driven. It ain't natural."

"Hold on there. What exactly is the ego?"

"The ego is a genetic invention that makes you separate yourself from the environment. The ego is what makes you think you are an individual separate from everything and everyone else. The ego is what you think is your true self. But nothin' could be further from the truth."

"I'm getting angry now. Why would God, or whoever created the world, do this to us? Why would God genetically program us to be a mystery to ourselves?"

"I don't know. It makes no sense, does it?"

"No."

"Shunryu Suzuki would tell us to shut up, enjoy the present moment, and drink our delicious Hefeweizen."

Maddy laughed. It felt good to laugh. "Does that end our lecture for today?"

Aaron shrugged good-naturedly. "We can continue the lecture as long as we don't lose our peace over it."

"Okay. Let's continue on."

"The key is to take the energy used to satisfy the primary biological drives and redirect it toward the fundamental spiritual truths of love, freedom, and peace. Love is the experience of feelin' connected to everything and everyone. It's the experience of feelin' at one with everything and everyone. Anything that makes you feel separate is not in the service of love."

"The ego makes me feel separate."

"Precisely, Grasshopper." Aaron giggled. "Did you ever watch *Kung Fu?*"

Maddy rolled her eyes. "Of course!"

"I loved that show. There was a lot of wisdom there." Aaron drained the last of his beer. He waved to Joe. "Can we get another?"

Joe waved back. "Sure. I'm on my way."

Aaron looked back at Maddy. "Freedom is the experience of infinity, of havin' no limitations. Anything that makes you feel small or limited is not in the service of freedom."

"Again, the ego."

"Yup. When you don't get what you want, the ego starts to scream and yell. You feel pretty small and constricted when your desires are left unfulfilled."

Joe placed two more pints of Hefeweizen on the bar. "These are on me. Enjoy!"

Aaron nodded and a wide smile spread across his face. "Well, thanks, Joe. That's mighty kind of you." He turned back to Maddy. "And peace is the experience of complete contentment. In peace, you have no desire to be anyone other than yourself. That means you're happy where you are and you're happy with what you're doin'. Anything that detracts from that contentment is not in the service of peace."

Maddy smiled knowingly. "The ego."

Aaron nodded. "The ego is never satisfied for long. It always wants somethin' new and different." He paused and nodded with certitude. "We meditate in order to transcend the ego, in order to touch the love, freedom, and peace that lie deep within us. There's nothin' biological about these eternal truths."

"All right. I'm on board. But I've got to ask you a question. If you are trying to be spiritual, why do you drink beer and coffee, and smoke cigars, and hang out with wild women like me?"

Aaron looked at her. He was dead serious. "I don't try to be spiritual. I am spiritual. The cigars and beer and coffee and wild women like yourself are superficial add-ons. They're all just for fun. Just to pass the time. I'm not dependent on any of 'em to feel love, freedom, and peace. They're inside me already. They're inside me all the time. I feel 'em all the time."

Maddy's heart sank and her mouth went dry. Tears welled up in her eyes. "I'm just an add-on?"

"Maddy, until you stand in my shoes, you will never completely get what I'm sayin'. The shell that you call your body is the add-on. What you don't understand is that I see to the bottom of your soul and know who you really are. I love your true self. The rest is just an add-on. The rest is nothin' but a shell of fluctuatin' moods and thoughts and behaviors."

Maddy had some irrational trust in what Aaron was saying. "Well, hell, if you know me and love me for who I really am, then I don't have much to complain about, do I?"

"No. You shouldn't have any complaints at all."

Twenty minutes later, Aaron and Maddy stood in the parking lot outside the Harpoon Brewery. They looked up at the vastness of the clear, blue sky. Aaron nodded and smiled. "When your mind is like this open sky, stretchin' to infinity, encompassin' everything and nothin', you'll know what happiness is." He paused. "You'll know that what has to happen will happen. And you'll be okay with that."

Chapter 52

Walt Dropo slammed the door behind him. He was breathing heavily, and his brain buzzed with ambiguous anticipation. He took off his coat and draped it on the back of his chair. He leaned over his desk and grabbed the file on the prisoner. He held the file to his chest and stared into the empty, gray space of the office.

"Christ, Walt, where the hell have you been? Phone's been ringin' off the hook." Ned Neville stood in the doorway leading to the cells in the back. He was red in the face and clearly exasperated.

Walt looked at Ned and snarled. "Don't worry about me, Ned. You go on and paddle your own canoe."

"What?"

Walt brought the file down to his waist and stuck out his scrawny chest. His eyes burned with resentment. "Get on patrol, Ned. Do as I say."

Ned shrugged angrily and grabbed his coat off the back of his chair. He walked hurriedly to the door and then turned back as he opened it. "Fuck you, Walt! Fuck you!" He walked out, slamming the door behind him.

Walt stood behind his desk in a state of dizzy entropy. He felt a hot sweat simmering on his skin. A drunken smile appeared across his sallow face like a slow-moving, dark shadow. He didn't give a shit about anything. At least it felt that way. He liked the feeling. He snorted and marched back to the cells.

He had not been to the prisoner's cell since the day the one-armed man arrived. When was that? Yesterday? Yeah. Yesterday. He grabbed a straight-backed, wooden chair from a sidewall of the cellblock and placed it square in front of the prisoner's cell, some three feet from the dull gray, vertical bars. He hadn't looked at the prisoner one time. Didn't want to. Until now.

Walt sat on the chair, his back straight and taut. He raised his eyes and stared at the prisoner with cold apprehension.

The prisoner sat on a faded brown picnic bench in the center of the cell. His short, black hair bristled on the top of his head. A specter of clownish horror, his face was sculpted with cheekbones protruding sharply up and out beneath shadowy sockets housing black coal eyes sunk back deep into his skull. Narrow shoulders slumped down lazily. The space where his left arm should have been was like a black, empty shaft leading somewhere no one in his right mind would want to contemplate.

Walt breathed deeply and turned his head down to look at the file. He opened the plain manila folder and stared at the prisoner's identifying information. "Rickey Spivey. What the fuck kind of name is that?"

The prisoner glared at Walt from some cavernous, dark place. "It ain't any kinda name. Just Rickey Spivey." The prisoner's voice was low and gravelly, as if he'd just smoked a pack of unfiltered cigarettes. He paused, his face still as a death mask. "You got a problem with my name?"

Walt chewed his bottom lip. "I got a problem with everything about you."

"Is that so? And what are you gonna do about that? You gonna come in here with ol' Rickey? Ol' Rickey would like that."

Walt looked back down at the sheet of paper. "You just can't stay outta trouble, can you?" Walt stared at the prisoner with glassed-over, drunken eyes. "You got a rap sheet like I never ever seen. You like hurtin' people, don't you?"

The prisoner scratched his close-shorn scalp. He pursed his lips and spat on the floor. "I guess you could say that."

Walt squinted his eyes, closely studying the prisoner. He scuffed his boots back and forth on the floor. "I always liked Blake Stallone. But ever since I learned he took your arm, I like him even more. You could say he's a hero of mine."

The prisoner smiled darkly. "You like dead heroes? Is that what you like?" The prisoner stuck out his blood red tongue. "Or do you like your heroes in itty-bitty pieces? Maybe that's what you like."

Walt scanned the file again. "You come from Alabama. Hmmm. I like Alabama. How did a piece of shit like you ever come from Alabama?"

The prisoner raised his matted eyebrows. "I don't come from Alabama. Where I come from ain't on no map."

Walt smirked. "What are you then? Some kind of fuckin' alien? That would explain why you're so fuckin' stupid."

The prisoner smiled. He was dead calm. "I ain't no fuckin' alien. I'm as human as you are. The difference 'tween you and me is I ain't no fuckin' coward." The prisoner chortled. "I can smell your fear, my brother." He closed his eyes and inhaled deeply through his nose. "It smells like turpentine."

Walt frowned and felt his heart hammer in his chest. "I'd rather be full of fear than full of evil." Walt leaned back. He couldn't believe what he had just said.

"I'm just gonna call you Mr. Turpentine. You don't mind that, do you?" The prisoner gnawed at his bottom lip with his short, pointy teeth. "Evil? You mention evil? What the fuck do you know about evil?" The prisoner leaned his head back and squinted ominously. "Nobody knows evil like I do. Shit, I could be a Ph. fuckin' D. of evil." He shook his head dismissively. "God got many sides to him. You think bein' good puts you on the right side of God. Nothin' could be stupider than that. You think life is precious? Is that what you think? Hell, Mr. Turpentine, take a good, hard look at life. It's nothin' but a fuckin' massacre. Floods, earthquakes, plagues. Who the fuck you think brings that on? Huh? It's God. Who the fuck else could it be? And what about the animals in the jungle? Feedin' off one another. Who do you think brings that on?"

Walt picked at his fingernails. The booze was starting to wear off. He yelled, "What about you, shithead? Tell me about you!"

The prisoner pulled at his long, narrow nose with his only hand. "I just love talkin' about me. Glad you asked." He flared his nostrils. "I am God's courier of evil. That's what I am. Been that since I was a little boy. It ain't like I choose it. Nope. It's just the way I am." He studied Walt in silence. "It's like your fear, Mr. Turpentine. It ain't a choice. It's just who you are." The prisoner laughed. A scary, hyena laugh. "Who do you think brings that out in you? Huh? I wonder."

Walt's equilibrium was becoming skittish. "You're nothin' but a murderin' motherfucker. You're nothin' but shit. You make me sick!"

"What about you, Mr. Turpentine? You killed anybody? Huh? I know you ain't never done that. You ain't got it in you. But you think killin' somebody means makin' 'em dead. Shit, you killed plenty of people that are still walkin' around. You kill 'em with your weakness, your fear, your failure. I bet you got a wife at home who fuckin' hates you. I bet your deputy hates you. I already know that. I can tell. You think about it. What have you done to make this fuckin' world a better place? Huh? I bet you just leave a pile of shit wherever you go. You're nothin' but a loser. You kill people by just bein' around 'em. You kill their will to live." The prisoner spat on the floor. He nodded and smiled. "You're just like me, Mr. Turpentine. We just do our killin' in different ways."

Walt blinked hard, fighting back tears. He quickly got up and hurried away from the cells. Moments later, he stood shaking in front of his desk. He heard the prisoner yell, "Don't look to God for help! He made you who you are!" There was quiet. Then he heard the prisoner yell again. "Hey, Mr. Turpentine, who ever told you the truth like me? Huh? Nobody! That's for damn sure!" Walt sat down in his chair with a heavy thud. He stared into the recesses of his imploding mind, fitfully pondering what the prisoner had just said. Walt swallowed hard as the fear washed over him.

Chapter 53

Raymond Lessing stood on the bridge overlooking the waterfall. A dawn fog engulfed the Robert E. Lee Memorial Park in ghostly waves of white and pink, floating around him in a ballet of atmospheric necessity. The dreams of apparitional causation had haunted him throughout the night and driven him out of his bed and the uncertain future of further dreams to the park he had cherished as a child. He remembered with fondness the graceful innocence of hiking on the wooded paths and playing with the packs of dogs that gathered there in canine camaraderie. As he looked out to the east, the drifting haze reminded him of an apparitional veil, revealing faint, luminous streams of pink and silver. His intelligence told him the sun was behind it all, as real and necessary as could ever be, but his senses grasped everything but. He shook his head. The tomfoolery was palpable. *It is not that the external world is unreal,* he thought, *but that the real is not to be found in the external. So where is the real to be found? Within? Yes, the real is found inside oneself!* Raymond took a long, deep breath. He looked hard into the opalescent mist. Wanting to see the sun. Wanting to see the real. *My physical eyes cannot see what is real! They just don't have the capacity.* Raymond looked down at the icy shards of water crashing on the rocks below and billowing back up into fog and crystalline spray. *How do I see with the internal eye? Who can tell me?*

Chapter 54

Walt Dropo stared into his cup of cold coffee. He hadn't taken a single sip. Really didn't have a mind to. He looked up and glared at his wife sitting across from him. Chewing slowly and systematically like an old cow, she stared down into her bowl of Brigham's Fluffernutter ice cream. Her black patch was lodged over her left eye socket, but for the life of Walt Dropo, it looked like some deep, cavernous hole from which he longed to extricate himself. Walt looked at his Timex: 8:45 p.m. "Gotta go," he said. "Don't know when I'll be back."

Chapter 55

Walt Dropo sat in his Pontiac Bonneville about a block south of the police station. Situated on the opposite side of the street, he could see the light from the front window of the station spraying the sidewalk with a malevolent, metallic glare. He swallowed hard and tasted that metal in his mouth, his arrhythmic heart bumping along with moral uncertainty. He checked his Timex: 9:57 p.m. Suddenly, the station lights vanished and the dark of night hardened before him like some unwanted presence signaling that time had stopped and there was no avoidance to be claimed. Walt leaned back in his seat and watched Ned Neville come out of the station and lock the door behind him. His mouth went dead dry as he watched Ned walk a little ways north on Jefferson Street, cross over to the other side, and get into his Buick LaCrosse. As the Buick's red taillights disappeared into the night's black cold, Walt opened his car door and got out.

When he got to the prisoner's cell, the thoughts in his fevered brain were banging around like errant ping-pong balls. The overhead fluorescent light in the cellblock flickered spasmodically like a cipher signaling some monstrous ambiguity was at hand.

Walt stared in catatonic disquietude at the prisoner. Spivey was lying on an old cot, his head raised at a slight angle on a doubled-up pillow. In the wavering light, he looked like some discarded madman who should be avoided at all costs. "Well, look what the cat drug in," said the murderer in an eerie Southern drawl that wasn't there the day before.

"Get up."

"Get up? I just damn near lied down. Why would I wanna get up?"

"'Cause I *told* you to get up!"

Spivey took a long, exasperated breath. "You don't mean shit to me. I'm stayin' right here."

Walt calmly unzipped his leather jacket and pulled from the waist of his pants an M9 semi-automatic pistol. Out of his jacket pocket, he retrieved a 15-round magazine loaded with 9mm cartridges. He smiled to himself as he installed the magazine.

At the sight of the weapon, Spivey started to laugh. "Ah, come on now, Mr. Turpentine. What do you plan to do with that little toy? You gonna shoot me?"

Boom! An ear-lancing explosion rang out in the cellblock as a flash of silver light darted into empty space. The bullet lodged itself in Spivey's right thigh. Spivey's leg jumped spasmodically for a few seconds and then settled down. He raised his head up off the pillow, grunting and giggling like some poor, dumb urchin who preferred staying in the hellhole into which he was born. "Ah, Mr. Turpentine. You tryin' to deliver a message to ol' Rickey? Is that what you're tryin' to do?"

Boom! Another deafening crack and brilliant flare exploded through the cell bars. Spivey's left leg started jerking around like a hooked mackerel. Then the leg settled down.

Walt stood there wondering about Spivey's legs. Although Spivey's body responded to the bullets searing into its flesh, it was as if the pain didn't register in Spivey's brain. He just lay there, moving his head up and down, laughing and giggling like a deranged clown in a traveling sideshow of freaks and misfits.

Spivey's face began to swell, the veins, like worn rope, protruding at his temples. His laughter was not human. "Now hold on just a minute, Mr. Turpentine. Just hold your horses." Spivey pushed himself up on his forearm and braced himself in that posture. "If you think killin' me is gonna absolve you from your worthless, cowardly life, well, you're just flat-out *wrong*." Spivey arched his eyebrows until they disappeared into the loose skin of his forehead. "Hell, man, are you that stupid? Don't you know that *you are what you are?* Don't you know that? And nothin' you do is gonna help you escape from yourself! Nothin'!"

Boom! Spivey fell back hard, his right arm a thrashing contortion until mercifully spent. His stomach convulsed in waves. His breathing was labored, but he kept on laughing in sporadic, loud outbursts. "Wooo, boy! You're into it now, ain't you, Mr. Turpentine? Wait! Wait! What is that I smell? Wait! Why, it's fear! It's *your* fuckin' fear!"

Walt felt as if his head were about to implode. His mouth involuntarily twisted to the side of his face. He wanted to speak but couldn't. He studied the macabre body lying on the cot like some frozen emotion that God had decided not to let loose on the denizens of the earth.

Then the body rose, straight up from the waist, mocking the agonized sheriff in the kaleidoscopic show of flickering fluorescence. Black blood streamed onto the mattress and floor, gleaming ominously in the heckling light. Spivey's face was calm but misshapen, like a piece of fruit that has turned and become soft. "My, oh, my. You have gone and done it now." Spivey's speech harangued Walt in loud bursts, with the most haunting of silences in between. "You have secured your legacy. Yes, sir."

Silence.

"You may *think* you are doin' God's will! You may *think* that!"

Silence.

"But you don't *know* that! You, Mr. Turpentine, have not been blessed with mental acumen. No, sir."

Silence.

"You have *shit* for brains. In fact, I can't reckon why I'm even tryin' to help you see what you cannot *possibly* see."

Silence.

"But I will persevere. I will persevere."

Silence.

"I *know* you are doin' the will of God. I *know* it. 'Cause I am *close* to God. I *hear* his voice inside me."

Silence.

"I *know* who I am. I *know* who you are. I see the divine plan unfoldin' in its utter perfection and can *tolerate* it! *Endure* it!"

Silence.

"But you are dumb as a rock. You are one of the vast mass of creatures that God uses as unconscious puppets. I pity you, Mr. Turpentine, I pity you."

Silence.

"Did you know that there are couriers of God who have my acumen, and yet play an entirely different part in life's grand drama? Did you know that? Did you know that those couriers are strivin' to balance the playin' field? To combat those who are like me? Yes. They are there. Amongst you."

Silence.

"But, alas, you will never know this."

Boom! Spivey's body lay quiet. In the trembling light. In the cold cell riddled with blood and urine and feces.

Then his head rose. Straight up from the neck. His black, dead eyes locked in some otherworldly trance. His mouth opened. "You have gone and killed a *knowin'* courier of God. One of the few. And you *think* you are now saved. You *think* you are redeemed. Well, think again. Think again."

Boom!

~ ~ ~ ~ ~

By 5:00 a.m., he had crossed into Pennsylvania, heading west on Route 84. Earlier, he had filled up on flapjacks and coffee at an all-night truck stop. Now he drove steadily, listening to Willie Nelson through the fitful static on the radio.

On...road again...

He turned his head and looked off to the east, hoping to see a glimmer of light. But there was none. All night long he wondered if he would ever see the sunrise again. He wondered what the daytime would look like hundreds of miles away from his hellish life in Halfmoon.

Goin' places...never been...

He leaned over to the passenger's seat and took a cigarette from his pack of unfiltered Camels. He tapped the cigarette on the steering wheel and put it between his lips. Then he retrieved his Zippo lighter from the breast pocket of his flannel shirt. He lit up and sucked the chalky smoke deep into his lungs. He felt his heart bump and then relax into a lazy, steady rhythm. He exhaled and watched the smoke rise before his eyes like a mysterious veil of trickery and deception. He smiled and felt better than he had for many a year.

Chapter 56

Aaron Riley sat down on his haunches and examined the excrement. He looked up at Maddy. "This is bear dung. We need to be vigilant." He got up and stretched his back and looked up the side of the mountain. "I think we'll be fine if we stick to the trail."

They hiked up the mountainside, through snow and brush and shallow thicket, and reached a plateau stretching out over rock where the light had forged through a clearing in the canopy of evergreens. The sun was warm on the backs of their necks, and their legs carried a heaviness that burned their thighs. They stopped and rested on a small ledge cantilevered above a valley of pine and birch. A granite quarry glistened in the distance. They sat on the craggy shelf with their legs stretched out and drank bottled spring water. Aaron leaned his head back and let the sun soak into his cheeks and forehead.

"The spiritual life starts with a retreat from the desires of biological necessity. It culminates with the death of the ego." Aaron winked at Maddy and continued. "Our desires for food, sleep, sex, and self-preservation must be completely stripped to their barest essences. We want to weaken their strength as much as possible. In that way, the mind has a chance of linkin' with what's real and experiencin' love, freedom, and peace. You see, the longer the mind stays away from the biological demands, the more it can concentrate on the real. It'll do it naturally. But once the biological necessity is fulfilled, the mind loses all its desire to seek the real. It's like a burned-out motor. So the deal is this: Eat very little. Eat organic. Eat just enough to stay healthy and fit. And don't obsess over the eating ritual. Then all that conserved energy can be used by the mind to direct itself toward the real. Next, sleep only when you're tired. And don't make a big deal over special linens and mattresses and nightgowns and other sleeping paraphernalia. Just curl up and sleep. The less energy you put into the fanfare of sleep, the more energy the mind will have to concentrate on the real."

Maddy held up her hand. "Time out. What exactly is the real?"

"The real is the source. That from which the cosmos appears. It's pure presence. Some people call it God." Aaron squinted and shook his head contrarily. "I'd rather not use that word. It's the source of too much conflict."

Maddy stared at Aaron with a signature of confusion on her face.

"In deep meditative states, you'll experience the real. But the mind doesn't have the energy to do it if it's burned out by the pull of the biological necessities."

Maddy nodded. "Go on."

"Next, the sexual act should not be at all contrived or stylized. It should just happen. Naturally. In the present moment." Aaron smiled mischievously. "The problem is this: Once you orgasm, the mind is completely shot. It has no energy with which to seek the real." Aaron paused. "And this is very important: if sex dominates your life and overwhelms your mind, you have no chance."

Maddy rolled her eyes. "Hmmm."

"Finally, the selfish desire for your own welfare needs to be mellowed. It's really a matter of tweakin' your perspective. The best way to do it is to put the welfare of others before your own. Always be willin' to sacrifice your own comfort to help someone else. In this way, the strength of the ego is diminished."

"So we should divert our energy away from meeting the needs of biological necessity and channel it toward seeking the real."

"Precisely. That's sadhana. When the mind merges with the real, love, freedom, and peace will blossom in your heart."

"Is that what enlightenment is?"

Aaron looked out over the snow-covered valley. "Yeah. I guess so. And once it strikes, it's permanent. It leaves an indelible impression on the mind." Aaron laughed mischievously. "Once that enlightenment strikes, you can have all the beer and cigars you want. They just won't affect you anymore. You can take 'em or leave 'em." Aaron looked at Maddy with compassion. "I must tell you that enlightenment is very rare. We have to go against a strong biological current to reach the shore of wisdom. The problem is this: every time we fulfill a desire of biological necessity, that desire becomes stronger. That's why it's so important to renounce those desires and redirect the mind toward the real."

Maddy smiled sadly. "I'm afraid I'm really behind the eightball."

"We all are. In the end, enlightenment is not somethin' that we can make happen. It's somethin' that happens to us."

"Why should we even try?"

"Because some of us are destined to try." Aaron shrugged. "Go figure."

Chapter 57

February 10, 2001

Dear Ray,

I have been haunted lately by memories of our youth. You and I were once engaged in the meaningfulness of things. You, with your subatomic physics and quantum mechanics; me, with my existentialism and phenomenology. What has happened to us? Why have we failed so miserably? Is it that we wanted to say dangerous things? That we wanted to move people into the realm of truth—a realm for which they were not ready? I think that's it. The world is not ready for the truth.

I am ready for the truth! I want it to crush me and make me wail for deliverance. That's why I live in a cave in Bali. That's why I meditate eight hours a day and subsist on nothing but rice, lentils, and goat's milk. That's why I put up with the giant spiders and beetles and wasps and snakes. —Did you know that not far from here, on the island of Komodo, are the Komodo dragons (descendents of prehistoric lizards)? They grow to be ten feet in length and can weigh as much as three hundred pounds. They roam the landscape, hunting their prey, which include humans, deer, goats, and water buffalo. If their initial attack doesn't kill you, the toxin in their saliva will! —I am in no man's land. This is the land of truth. This is the place where those who are ready for the truth must come.

Ray, something has happened to me. I will try my best to recount it, but, alas, it's not the stuff words can convey. I'm living through an emotional upheaval. I'm so sensitive: my bones literally ache with compassion, and I feel like weeping at the drop of a hat. The long and the short of it is this: When I was in a deep state of meditation, my guru placed his hand on the crown of my head and chanted an esoteric mantram. Ray, it was as if I were struck by lightning. My entire being shattered into a thousand points of light—flickering brightly and then dying away like an apocalyptic finale at a fireworks display. I literally saw every scene of my life pass before me. I was devoured simultaneously by unspeakable joy and suffering. I do not exaggerate when I say that every atom of my mind and body was sucked out of me and rendered useless. I am dead, Ray. Dead but somehow alive.

I am told the aching bones and the tears will dissipate with time—it is the aftermath of being torn asunder and rendered useless. I feel like an instrument in the hands of God. I have no will of my own.

There is a line in a poem by Eleh Ezkerah: "'Tis a fearful thing to love what death can touch." I ask you: What is it on the finite plane of human existence that death cannot touch? Do you see the impasse? In the Hindu mystical tradition, we speak of the jivanmukta, the one who is liberated while still alive. It is said that the cool moon could rise at midday, or the dead could germinate from the graveyards and walk the earth, and the jivanmukta would not be at all surprised or in any way affected. The jivanmukta would accept the happenings and continue with his life. The jivanmukta knows that this life is merely the playground of God. Anything can happen. The energy of life is the source of infinite possibility, infinite potentiality. And the expression of the energy is always changing. That's why the mystics are not materialists. They never attach to the changing landscape of material forms.

Ray, the only answer to the call for spiritual survival is to get back to our original nature: the formlessness of infinitude. We must drop the finite mind and body like a corpse. This can be done only by turning inward so deeply that identification with our minds and bodies disappears. What is left is the formless energy of infinitude. The Buddhists call this emptiness. Only emptiness can take the infinite variety of forms that we see in the world of space and time. Only emptiness can be the placeholder of the constantly changing forms. To be empty of form is to be free!

Your brother in renunciation,
Alex

Chapter 58

Walt Dropo finished his bacon and eggs and pushed the plate to the side. He cradled in his hands a hot cup of coffee in order to ward off the cold. The heating system in June's Midtown Restaurant was none too cooperative. Barbara-Jean said it was on the fritz. Barbara-Jean was the waitress at June's. Thirty-seven years old. Plump. Busty. Had curly-frizzy, blond hair that wrapped itself above her cute, cherubic face. She knew Walt as Frank. Just plain Frank. She took a shine to Frank.

Frank stared out the window onto Main Street. He wondered what spring would look like in Honesdale, Pennsylvania. Probably not much different from spring in Halfmoon. Frank nodded at Barbara-Jean, and she happily topped off his coffee. Frank had always wanted to go to the Poconos. He wasn't sure why that was the case. But that's where he ended up. The little town of Honesdale in the Lake Region of the Pocono Mountains.

Frank crossed his legs and breathed deeply. He felt good. He smiled to himself and chuckled. In Honesdale, two hundred thousand dollars could go a mighty long way.

Chapter 59

Between the bitter cold of snowy winter and the brisk, exhilarating revelation of spring is what Vermonters call mud season. It's when time beckons, but spring fails to arrive. It's when all the winter snow and ice marry with the dirt and gravel beneath, causing the country roads and pathways and turnabouts to deteriorate into sloppy, soupy, gritty mud that morphs into ruts and crater-like depressions when the temperatures drop below freezing in the bewitching darkness of night. Mud season is when the locals themselves don't dare to go far from home for fear of getting stuck in the mud that waits for them. Waits. Waits for them.

Matilda Dropo was *stuck*. Back on Elders Lane off Route 4. She had been to see Helen Biltmore, her best friend. She cried with her one eye, her head on Helen's shoulder. She cried again and some more about Walt. His up and leaving. His utter absence. His probable complicity in the shooting of that prisoner who killed Blake. Matilda Dropo was *stuck*.

She climbed out of her all-wheel-drive Subaru and stood off to the side of the road. It was dusk, and the wind was picking up, and no birds were singing. She looked up and down Elders Lane and saw nothing. An emptiness engulfed her, and it seemed to her as if time had stopped for all the world. Trying to walk home wasn't a consideration. Too far and too much mud and the darkness was rapidly approaching. She decided to just wait.

Wait for the next car or truck to pass through. Wait for somebody to help her.

The wind started to swirl with a power that unnerved her. The tall poplars and white aspens in the surrounding forest swayed and twisted ominously like playthings of an angry god. She heard a loud, crisp *crack* split the wall of sound configured by the winds reeling behind her. She twisted her body around and looked up, her one eye gaping, into the shifting shadows of evening grayness.

Chapter 60

Aaron Riley sipped his Bass Ale and crunched down on a handful of peanuts. "Did you hear about Matilda Dropo?"

Maddy looked up as she cleaned the surface of the bar with a damp rag. "No. What's going on with Matilda?"

Aaron shook his head. "She's dead. A tree fell on her out on Elders Lane."

Maddy felt her breath catch. She swallowed hard. "Oh, my God." She stood behind the bar in silence.

"A dead poplar came down on her. Apparently the wind took it down. Snapped the tree off about a third of the way up."

Maddy frowned. "That's what you call *bad* luck."

"That's for sure."

Maddy furrowed her brow. "Lots of bad luck seems to be finding its way to Halfmoon."

Aaron arched his eyebrows with some prescient knowledge. "Yeah. Seems that way."

Maddy leaned across the bar. "Have you heard anything about Walt?"

"No." Aaron paused in thought and then shook his head and smiled. "I think Walt is long gone. And I don't think the cops are lookin' that hard for him."

"Why do you say that?"

"I think the cops see Walt as some kind of hero. He had the balls to do what they wanted to do but couldn't." Aaron shrugged knowingly. "And I bet Walt feels good about it. In fact, I know he does."

Maddy nodded. "I've got to wait on some people. Catch you later."

"You bet." Aaron stroked his beard with circumspection, like a poet pondering a decisive phrase. He could see through his mind's eye that Walt had slain an inner demon when he killed that prisoner. *Yep. Walt's definitely feelin' better.*

Chapter 61

March, 20, 2001

Dear Alex,

It seems that your time in Bali is...is...hell, Alex, your letters sound like gibberish to me. What can I say? I sincerely hope you find whatever it is you're looking for.

It seems that Baltimore has little to offer me. Or perhaps I have little to offer Baltimore. At any rate, I'm going to close down the house here in Homeland and head for the farm in Halfmoon. Like you, I'm looking for something. Maybe the object of my quest is in Halfmoon. Maybe not. Only the future holds the promise or the disappointment.

Take care of yourself,
Ray

Chapter 62

Springtime in Vermont. The snow has melted. The mud has dried. The rivers are high. The daily temperatures swing along a thirty-degree arc. Sixty-degree days. Thirty-degree nights. The buds on the poplars and birches and aspens stand at the ready, waiting to burst into greenery when the warm air sees fit to hold.

Aaron and Maddy sat on a hill under a massive silver maple tree on the grounds of the Green Mountain Dharma Center. They looked down at the red meditation barn resting in the sun-drenched valley below. Aaron adjusted his Red Sox ball cap on his big, burly head. "When you meditate, and touch the sweet spot of your spirit, you know the power of stillness. Everything that's not still comes out of that stillness."

Maddy nodded. The bright sun made her squint. "You're right. I never thought of it that way. But when you touch that stillness within, you feel a tremendous power that's ordinarily latent."

"Yeah. The stillness is where the origin of things lies. That's the source for all the sound and fury of the world. It's important to never lose touch with that source."

Maddy winked. "Yeah. If you do, you start to believe that the sound and the fury is what's important."

Aaron smiled and laughed. "Yeah. And then you're *completely* fucked!"

Maddy gently kicked the hillside soil with the heel of her hiking boot. "That stillness within is nothing other than peace."

"Yeah. We should always be grounded in that peace."

Maddy pursed her lips in concentration. "You know, Aaron, I owe a lot to you. You've really opened my eyes to the proper way of living. I feel like I want to give something back. Share what I've learned with others."

Aaron shook his head dismissively. "The masses aren't ready for this wisdom, Maddy. Don't waste your time." He paused in thought, his eyes twinkling with prescient insight. "But I'll tell you what would be the right thing to do. We should start a Peacemaker Order. Right here in Halfmoon."

"What's a Peacemaker Order?"

"It's a spiritually based social-action organization founded by Bernie Glassman. Bernie's a Zen Master." Aaron nodded with conviction. "The members of the order go about doin' good. They help those in need. Those who are sufferin'. Those who can't help themselves. They demonstrate to the world the virtue of livin' peacefully, where every action and every thought is grounded in mindfulness." Aaron chuckled. "And they don't worry about proselytizin'. They already know there's no point in that." Aaron paused. "The thing is this: We can't wait for everyone to become enlightened. We have to get out there and serve humanity right now. We have to let our peaceful, sane actions speak for themselves and serve as examples for others to follow."

Maddy smiled as a warm breeze cascaded down the hillside. "Gosh, Aaron. I think your idea is just beautiful."

Aaron nodded, a wide smile spreading over his face. "Makes sense, doesn't it? Let's give it a whirl."

A quiet hillside in Hartland, Vermont. Two seekers come upon a course of action that makes the heavens sing.

Chapter 63

Walt Dropo sat in a lawn chair on the grassy shoreline of Lackawanna Lake. Next to him, within arm's reach, was a cooler filled with Budweiser. His hands lazily gripped his fishing rod, the line of which ran across the surface of the water and disappeared some twenty yards out into the vast, two-and-a-half-mile-long lake. At eight thirty in the morning, the sun hovered low on the horizon and surreptitiously sprayed a toasty warmth through the still, windless air.

Walt was hoping to catch some trout. Or maybe a big, old largemouth bass. *It'd be nice to cook up some fresh fish for Barbara-Jean,* he thought. He gazed out over the majestic expanse of water and thought about how surreal it looked. The lake's surface reminded him of a polished mirror. He studied the glasslike veneer of the still water and pondered the wispy white clouds reflected there. Alternating his attention between the clouds floating in the sky above and their reflection on the calm expanse of the lake, he thought of something he had read in the newspaper. Something about parallel universes. He wondered if there were such a thing.

Then he noticed the silence. A kind of silence that he had never heard before. A silence that wrapped itself around him like a pressurized chamber. He pushed up the brim of his ball cap and looked around. No people. No boats. No movement. No sound. He furrowed his brow and then chuckled. *Shit,* he thought, *this is damn strange.* He looked down at his new watch. The date read May 17, the time 8:32 a.m. He pulled down on the brim of his cap, got up from his lawn chair, and gently secured the handle and reel of his fishing rod to the metal armrest of the chair.

Sucking at the smooth membrane of his cheeks as he made his way leisurely down the couple of yards to the water's edge, Walt stopped and stretched his shoulders back and took a deep breath. He looked up and down and across the cove and considered the stillness. The stillness of the air. The stillness of the lake. The utter silence. The utter solitude. It occurred to him that he felt as if the first fifty years of his life had never happened. Memories were there if he cared to look at them. But they had no pull to them, no tension. He'd rather forget about it. All of it. He smiled like an old man might smile after living his life and accepting it and no longer feeling the need to go on. He felt like he'd been given a second chance. Why? He did not know. Nor did he care. And who dispensed this gift? He did not know. Nor did he care.

He walked back to his lawn chair, reclaimed his fishing rod, and sat back down. He leaned over to the right and grabbed a can of Budweiser from the cooler. Securing the can snugly between his thighs, he popped the top. With a silent toast to the mystery-laden universe, he raised the can to his mouth and took a long slug. The frothy bitterness stung his tongue and lips. Then, a demonstrative wave of sound and movement washed over him. He heard birds singing around him. He saw birds flying before him. He heard children laughing behind him. He saw children running past him. He felt the tug of his fishing rod and the responding tension in his hands and wrists. He felt an uncanny stillness at the center of his being. He smiled as an old man might smile after living his life and accepting it and no longer feeling the need to go on.

Chapter 64

Raymond Lessing stood on the expansive deck of his stylish post-and-beam farmhouse. As the sun set, stretching its light across the zenith of the evergreen tree line above him, he looked down into a valley of poplar and birch and pine. Colorful finches and hummingbirds were darting about, looking for seeds and insects. Raymond's gaze gravitated to a solitary gold and white warbler perched peacefully on a branch of a white birch some twenty yards away. He studied the bird for some time and got the sense that the warbler could see into the future. As if it were still enough to do so. As if it were detached enough to do so.

Raymond had been at the farmhouse for about two weeks. Puttering. Hiking. Sleeping. Pretty much being a lazy recluse. No one save the postmaster and the clerk at the local farmer's market knew he was there. And that was fine with him.

He wondered about his brother. Wondered when he might see him again. Wondered if they would connect. He thought about Dr. Bevis and felt embarrassed by the time he'd spent at Sheppard Pratt. Time. It waits for no one. Sometimes you just have to give in to time. Let what must be run its course. Psychology. An inexact science at best. An odd scenario: a shrink separates himself from the rest of humanity and then analyzes and evaluates what he deems he is no longer part of. Hmmm. And then there's the prescription regimen. It no doubt works for some afflictions. But care must be taken not to prescribe with knee-jerk reaction. Medication can very well complicate whatever it was that brought you to the shrink in the first place. It can act like a smokescreen that camouflages the affliction. Make it look different. Make it look not as bad. That's when the pills themselves become demons. Demons that hook their tentacles in you and make you dependent on something alien to the body.

Hell, straightening out your life is hit or miss. You either come by the light that takes you out of the darkness or you don't. And there's little rhyme or reason to any of it. Time. Time might be the answer. If we're lucky enough to have time on our side, some psychic wounds will heal on their own. The mind. So powerful. So fragile. When the mind no longer sees the need to hold on to the pain is when the healing begins.

Ray was healed. He could feel it. It was as if he never spent a single day in Sheppard Pratt. Or more correctly, whoever it was who went through that ordeal was no longer around. Couldn't be found anywhere. He knew he was lucky. Somehow he had survived his sessions with Dr. Bevis, sessions of repetitive dwelling on an open mental wound. Ray smiled sadly to himself and thought of Alexander sitting in a cave in Bali, longing for the shore beyond madness. Would Alexander have luck on his side?

Out of the corner of his right eye, Ray caught some movement where the forest line met the dirt driveway by the side of the house. There, to his happy surprise, was a huge black and white turkey. It strutted rhythmically toward the deck, its pink, wrinkled head and neck bobbing up and down as it moved through the country stillness. Easing to a halt in front of Ray, the ample wildfowl focused on him pointedly with tiny, red eyes. Uncomplicated eyes. But they made contact. They *acknowledged* Ray. Ray didn't say or do anything. He just remained still, making eye contact with the big, bulky bird. They stared at each other for a long time. Ray's mind was in a state of anticipatory receptivity. The present moment was filled to capacity and was quite satisfying in an odd kind of way. The bird cocked its narrow, sculpted head as if it were determining whether or not what had to happen, had happened. Seemingly satisfied that fate had run its course, the black-and-white-feathered creature strutted off into the woods and disappeared. Ray smiled and shook his head. This is country living. Encounters are made. And silence is acceptable. No, preferable. Silence is preferable. Ray thought about that for a moment and nodded knowingly. To break the silence is to infuse the unnecessary into what is already sublime.

Chapter 65

June 1, 2001

Dear Ray,

Bless you, my brother.

My blessing. Does it even reach your ears? Can it be assimilated in the shadowy muck of crass ignorance that spreads through the masses like some unabated cancer? I am alone with my prescience. I am like an undiscovered, holy crystal in a landscape of spiritual poverty.

It is the bloody, sad truth. A few weeks ago, I met James Guthrie, an eighty-year-old, retired theology professor from Rutgers, who is writing a book on the development of the eclectic religious culture that has managed to flourish here in Bali. He was directed to me because I'm the only one around here who speaks English. Last night, James got hold of a Jeep and we took a ride into Ubud. We went to this bar at the edge of the Monkey Forest and proceeded to embark on an enjoyable evening of conversation, sitting outside in the moonlight, drinking Absolut straight with rocks. I hadn't had any alcohol since I got here and was enjoying myself immensely. I was wearing my sannyasin garb (the traditional robe of the Asian monk), and James was wearing a black, sleeveless T-shirt and madras shorts. The monkeys were howling faintly in the distance, and all seemed right with the world. After a couple of rounds, the owner of the bar came out to say hello to James, whom he evidently knew. The owner, a Mexican (I kid you not!), chatted with us for a couple of minutes—and then, all of a sudden, he prostrated himself at my feet and started chanting, OMMMM, OMMMM, OMMMM.

Well, my God, I thought James was going to have a stroke! He started laughing and wailing hysterically, his arms and legs flailing in his rickety wicker chair. And then, the Mexican at my feet began rolling on the ground, laughing hysterically, holding his belly and grimacing to catch his breath.

My God, I was embarrassed. Humiliated. Nothingness engulfed me. But then, as if by a strike of lightning, the indisputable truth surged through every cell of my body. I saw myself—perhaps for the first time.

I am a rare jewel! An ambassador of God on earth. A mouthpiece for truth in a world choked by unforgiving ignorance.

At the precise moment of this self-revelation, the Mexican lifted himself off the ground, brushed off his pants and shirt, and said to me with what he thought was prescient kindness, "You're not the first person to come to Bali in search of himself. If you take yourself a little less seriously, you may find what you're looking for."

Ray, the Mexican couldn't be more wrong. I have to take myself seriously! I have to pound away at my ego until it is crushed to dust. No one understands this. No one.

I'm coming home to Vermont in a few months. I can see that the world needs me. Even if it's not ready for me.

Your brother, alone in the howling wilderness,
Alex

Chapter 66

Ray Lessing sat in his Dodge Ram pickup in the parking lot of the Elk Head Saloon. The sun sprayed streaks of orange and pink along the jagged, gray-shadowed crest of Wolf Mountain off to the west. Night was coming on and the crickets and frogs were lending a shimmering, humming undertone to the country silence. Ray nodded with conviction and got out of the truck.

When he walked into the saloon, it was just as he had remembered it. Cozy. Unobtrusive. Friendly. As he advanced toward the bar, the patrons making up the hearty crowd welcomed him with their nods, but no one recognized him. And that was fine with Ray.

Ray had been holed up at the farmhouse for a good month. And now he was ready to come back to the fold, ready to join the human race without pretense. Pretense. He just didn't have it in him anymore. Thank God. Ray slid up on one of the barstools and glanced to the right at the TV hanging on the back bar wall. Red Sox 2, Orioles 0. Bottom of the sixth. Ray felt his left arm being squeezed with affection. Turning his head back to the left, he was met eye to eye with a mountain of a man whom he did not recognize. The man had a heavy, graying beard and was smiling heartily. Ray tilted his head back to get a better look. He considered the face momentarily and nodded slowly. "I know you, don't I?"

The man gave Ray's arm another affectionate squeeze and then let go. "You sure do, Ray."

Ray's eyes opened wide at the recognition of the gravelly, down-home voice. "Well, I'll be damned. Aaron Riley. How are you, Aaron?"

Aaron's eyes twinkled with happy expectation. "I'm just fine, Ray. Just fine." Aaron shook his head in wonder. "You just never know who you're gonna see at the Elk Head. You just never know." Aaron took a sip of Long Trail Ale and smacked his lips. "How long have you been in Halfmoon?"

"About a month."

"A month? It's taken you this long to show yourself?"

"Yeah. That's true." Ray paused in reflection. "I really wasn't ready for meeting and greeting."

Aaron laughed. "Ten-four, good buddy."

Ray smiled good-naturedly. "I haven't heard that lingo in many a year."

Aaron opened his eyes wide, mocking Ray. "Well, then, you ain't been in Halfmoon for many a year."

Ray shrugged and pursed his lips. "Very true."

"Can I buy you a beer, Ray?"

Ray thought about it and decided against it. "You know, Aaron, I'm going to pass on the beer. I haven't had a drink since I was institutionalized. I feel a lot better when I stay away from the sauce."

"Can I buy you an orange juice?"

Ray nodded. "That would be kind of you. Thanks."

Aaron gave a yell down to the end of the bar. "Hey, Maddy. Can I get an OJ up here? When you get the chance?"

Maddy looked up and smiled and winked at Aaron.

Aaron turned to Ray. "OJ comin' up." He thoughtfully stroked his bushy beard. "What was it like in Sheppard Pratt? That is, if you don't mind me askin'."

Ray chuckled. "I don't mind talking about it. What exactly would you like to know?"

Maddy placed a glass of cold orange juice in front of Aaron and leaned across the bar. "I didn't know you mixed OJ and beer." She smiled coquettishly.

Aaron flipped her a wry smile and cocked his head toward Ray. "It ain't for me, Maddy. It's for my good buddy here."

Maddy nodded. "I stand corrected." She slid the glass of OJ in front of Ray.

"You don't recognize him, do you?"

Maddy studied Ray for a few moments. She screwed up her face in contemplation. She smiled. "Is that you, Ray?"

Ray shrugged, a little embarrassed. "Yep. It's me."

Maddy smiled widely and nodded demonstratively. "Well, good to see you, Ray. It's been a long time."

"Yeah. Too long."

"You gonna stay awhile?"

"I think I just might. We'll see."

"Well, that's just great." Cries for Maddy wafted through the chattering barroom. "Gotta run. Catch up with you later."

"Okay, Maddy. See you later." Ray smiled and sipped his OJ. In some odd way, he felt as if he were home. Not home in a geographical sense, but home as a spiritual anchor affording his mind and body happy respite. Ray looked at Aaron. "So where were we?"

"The loony bin," said Aaron ironically.

"Ah, yes. The loony bin." Ray raised his eyebrows quizzically. "I don't know what to say other than the docs are quick to dispense drugs and quick to force conversation that in the long run can be more crippling than edifying."

Aaron shrugged knowingly. "Doesn't surprise me. I've always had my doubts about the psychiatric community." He studied Ray momentarily. "But you're feelin' better now?"

"Yeah. I'm okay."

"That's good." Aaron took a slug of ale. "What do you hear from Alex?"

Ray winced and then smiled halfheartedly. "Alex is coming home. At least that's what he said in his last letter."

"Hmmm. He told me he was goin' to Bali to find himself." Aaron smirked. "Well, did he find himself?"

Ray sat straight up and stretched his shoulders. "Hell if I know. His letters are pretty fucked up. He's living in a cave. Trying to cross to the other shore. The shore beyond madness."

Aaron's eyebrows popped up. "The other shore? The one beyond madness? Hmmm. To each his own."

"Yeah. To each his own." Ray stared at his glass of orange juice. The glass sweated cold beads of pearly condensation. "Heck, Aaron, I'm a good one to stand in judgment. I just got out of the loony bin."

Aaron nodded and considered the remark. "How did you get out? How did you survive the drugs and forced conversation?"

Ray clasped his hands together and leaned forward on the bar. The pose he struck was not prayerful. "I was lucky. Some part of me must have resisted the drugs because I made a conscious decision not to ingest them. After a couple of months, my mind cleared." Ray sat silent, wondering if he should reveal the next bit of information. He nodded decisively. "And then something interesting happened. I started to dream."

"Dream?"

"Yeah. Dreams came to me in my sleep. Actually, they were more like messages than dreams."

"Messages?"

"Yeah." Ray looked at Aaron solemnly. "I think they were messages from God." Ray shook his head and swallowed hard. "I'm no religious fanatic. In fact, I'm not into any kind of God worship. But I'll tell you, I think these were messages from God."

Aaron pursed his lips. "Hmmm. Tell me more."

"These messages were scientific. They were about the origin of the cosmos. I think they were sent to me because my mind was one of the few that could understand it. I don't know if you remember anything about my background, but I was considered to be the next Einstein within the Cal Tech circle. For some reason, though, I didn't catch on. I still don't know why."

"The forces of nature are inscrutable. They push and pull and don't wait for us to understand. That's the long and the short of it."

Ray nodded and then chuckled with relief.

"Tell me about the messages, Ray. I'm interested."

Ray paused a moment and then decided to continue. "Well, I think my mind was being used somewhat like an electronic receiver. The dream message came to me like a series of radio waves. And it wasn't as if what was received was up for discussion. It was just there, like a blueprint of creation." Ray inhaled deeply and continued. "The message boiled down to this: The world we experience is a product of apparitional causation. What we experience is not real. It is an illusion based on a mistake in perception. The irony is that we cannot help but make the mistake. We're wired to see the world incorrectly, to perceive it within space and time. And when we see the world within space and time, we can discern only the illusion. And when we respond to the illusion, it fucks us up. That's why none of us is truly happy. The illusion isn't satisfying. It doesn't fulfill our real needs. Only connecting with reality will fulfill our real needs."

Aaron's brain sizzled like a live wire. "Slow down for me, Ray. Let's just take this nice and easy. You're sayin' that from the start, we're doomed to experience unhappiness. You're sayin' we're wired to chase after an illusion. And that the only way we can experience the real is by goin' against our wirin'."

"That's it. You got it. Somehow, we have to cheat the genetic programming."

At the sound of that apocalyptic phrase, *cheat the genetic programming*, Aaron's throat tightened with emotion. He took a long, concentrated breath. He leaned close to Ray and whispered, "Ray, I got somethin' to tell you. But it's gonna take a while. Can you stay?"

Ray sensed the seriousness of the moment. "Sure, Aaron. I'll stay."

Chapter 67

Frank held Barbara–Jean's hand with a gentleness that spoke of adoration. He felt as if he were in high school, on a date with his dream girl. Love is funny that way. It takes you outside of yourself, outside of all practical reckoning of place and time and generation. It's a mysterious emotion.

Frank knew he was in love. Didn't question it. Didn't fear the loss of it. Just went with it. He whispered to her, "It's nice sittin' here on the porch with you, Barbara-Jean. It's like I don't need much more to be happy."

Barbara-Jean leaned her wide, frizzy-haired head on Frank's scrawny shoulder. "It's good bein' with you, Frank."

"Sometimes I feel like a miracle's happened. Like my world changed in the blink of an eye. Like one life came to an end and another started. And the one that started was nothin' at all like the one that ended."

Barbara-Jean squeezed Frank's hand with purpose and sat up next to him. She turned her face to his. "I got somethin' to tell you, honey. And I don't want you to worry. Can you promise me you won't worry?"

Frank sat at attention. "You ain't sick, are you?"

Barbara-Jean smiled and shook her head. "No, honey. It ain't nothin' like that." She pursed her lips and squinted. "I got a cousin in law enforcement. Up in Albany."

Frank's heart stopped on a dime. He felt faint and clammy. He licked his dry lips. "In Albany, you say?"

"Yeah. In Albany. You know him. Matt Lawlor's his name."

Frank's mouth twisted to the side, his eyes frozen still. "Yeah. I know Matt."

"Small world, ain't it?"

Frank's crippled nod registered the shock. "Too small, maybe."

"I told you not to worry, sweet pea. You've got nothin' at all to worry about. Matt ain't gonna say nothin'."

"How'd you come to know who I am?"

"Me and Matt have always been tight. Since we were little kids livin' in Buckingham, Virginia. A couple weeks ago, we were talkin' on the phone, and he was tellin' me about this sheriff in Vermont and how he killed this prisoner and how he disappeared and how no lawman in his right mind would ever turn him in."

Frank cocked his head. "That don't explain how you come to know it was me."

Barbara-Jean smiled and wrinkled her nose. "It was really just serenditty. Is that the word? Serenditty? Like when somethin' is made known completely by accident or luck?"

"Sounds right. I guess."

"Well, that's how it happened. I was tellin' Matt about this drifter who come into town back in March and how I took a likin' to him and how we got together. And I was describin' him, and Matt started askin' some questions, and the next thing you know, Matt says, 'I know Frank. I know who he is.'"

Frank slumped and he shook his head warily. "What are you gonna do, Barbara-Jean?"

"I'm gonna love you, Frank. That's all I'm gonna do."

"Are you sure about that? I understand if you wanna back off. I understand."

Barbara-Jean ran her plump hand along Frank's inner thigh. "Just gonna love you, Frank. That's all I'm gonna do."

Frank leaned back in the porch swing and took a deep breath. He looked out into the dark night sky and saw that the planets were rightly aligned. He felt Barbara-Jean's experienced hand on his member, and as it rose to meet her attentions, he saw shooting stars crossing in the infinite blackness above him like silver arrows migrating on ancient firmaments.

Chapter 68

Ray swallowed his orange juice and discreetly leaned toward Aaron. "Aliens? You really think you were abducted by aliens?"

Aaron shrugged nonchalantly. He had thought through all of this a thousand times. "Yeah. That's what I think. How else could I be completely transformed within a matter of hours? How else could I possess the wisdom? How else could I have the powers?" Aaron winked at Ray. "If you got a better answer, I wanna hear it."

Ray shook his head. "Fucking strange, isn't it?"

"That it is, my friend. That it is." Aaron took the last bite of his cheeseburger and washed it down with his ale. "Ray, what I've told you stays here with us. You and Maddy and me. We're the only ones who know."

"No problem."

"I'm serious. You can't even tell your brother."

"Okay."

Aaron pursed his lips in concentration. "You ready for the rest of my story? I think you'll find it interestin'."

"Sure, Aaron. Go on."

"You know how your message from God presented you with the keys to understandin' the origin of the cosmos? And how it explains that we're condemned to unhappiness?"

Ray nodded.

"And how it tells you that you gotta cheat the genetic programmin', and yet doesn't tell you how?"

"Yeah."

"Well, the aliens came at me with just the opposite torque. They told me how to cheat the genes, but they didn't fuckin' tell me why I had to do it. They didn't tell me about apparitional causation." Aaron smiled and flicked his tongue across his bottom lip. "Don't you find it kinda strange that you and me are sittin' here in Halfmoon, Vermont, in a bar in the fuckin' woods, and we get to talkin'—and, lo, we got the whole picture of truth and wisdom dead in our sights?" Aaron continued licking his bottom lip. "Look around here. Look at these fuckin' people. Do you think it would matter one iota if we stood up and explained the whole picture to 'em? Do you think they would hear one fuckin' word? I don't think so! No. I don't think so!"

Ray's eyes were bugging out in anticipation. "Aaron. Just hold on here. You've got to tell me how to cheat the genes." He stared at Aaron and nodded. "Then we'll consider spreading the word to the masses."

Aaron paused momentarily and shook his head. "You're right, Ray. I'm gettin' way ahead of myself. Sorry."

"Go on. Tell me about cheating the genes."

"Ray, it's all about the biological necessities that drive us to seek the illusion. It's all about eatin', sleepin', sex, and self-preservation. As long as we exhaust our energies dealin' with the biological necessities, the mind has no fuel left to seek the real. The longer we delay our gratification from eatin', sleepin', fuckin' and self-preservin', the better chance we have of connectin' up with the real. The real is the source. The real is what gives rise to the illusion. And Ray, the key to it all is the stillness that exists deep within you. That's what we want to touch. That's the source. You get there through the practice of meditation."

In his excitement, Ray thought he was going to fly off his chair. "Aaron, that's it. That's it. The message from God that was communicated to me said that we're wired to find the solution to every problem through action. Through movement. Through change. But all that does is strengthen the illusion of transformational causation."

Aaron cocked his head. "Transformational causation?"

"Yeah. Everything that exists within space and time is the product of transformational causation. One thing transforming into another. It's all based on the transformation of energy patterns. Transformation, or change, is the law of temporality." Ray held up the index finger of his right hand, signaling the imminent announcement of an apocalyptic insight. "But guess what you cannot get to through transformational causation? The source! The first cause! How the fuck can you get to the source through transformation? You can't. That's why the source must be beyond space and time. It can't be anywhere else. And what do you have when you transcend space and time? Stillness! No movement at all!"

Aaron squinted in thoughtful repose. "I believe you got it, good buddy. I believe that's a big ten-four."

"It's the granddaddy of ten-fours."

"Yeah. It is." Aaron rubbed his bushy beard and eyed the colorful, glassy landscape of the back bar. "The mind wants to get beyond space and time. It wants to experience peace and stillness. That's the state in which the mind is completely happy. But to get to that state requires an amazin' amount of concentration. Concentration that hones our consciousness down to an infinitesimal pinpoint. The problem is that we're wired to direct the energy of the mind outward toward fulfillin' the biological necessities. The only chance we have of redirectin' the mind inward toward the real is by cheatin' the genes." Aaron nodded with prescience. "That's what renunciation is. It's nothin' other than goin' against the wirin'. And it has to be that way if you want to connect with the real. See, the moment you gorge yourself with food, the mind has no desire to seek the real. It just sits there like a limp rag. And when you sleep for ten hours, same thing. And when you're constantly on the prowl for women and then get lucky, the mind just loses all interest in seekin' the real. It's just shot! The same for the desire for self-preservation, which is really just glorified narcissism. Yeah. That's the solution to the problem. We've gotta cheat the wirin'."

Ray stared into his empty glass. Bits of orange pulp lingered on the sides. He nodded. "So why do you think God orchestrated it this way? Seems kind of cruel, doesn't it?"

Aaron shook his head. "It does seem that way. But you know, there ain't no point in dwellin' on it. We're here in the middle of this shitstorm. And that's that."

Ray laughed and shrugged his shoulders. "And we really shouldn't try to do anything about it, should we? 'Cause that would just be more action and action isn't the answer. Stillness is the answer."

"Yeah. But we've gotta act. We can't stop actin'. Not as long as we're alive. What we've gotta do is act but remain still inside. That's what we've gotta do."

"And meditation is the process?"

"Yeah. Meditation will bring all the energy of the mind to a single point. And that's when you're really still." Aaron swirled the ale in his pint glass and watched it lacquer the sides. "Then we've gotta retain the stillness at all times and in all places. Then, when we act, we're really not actin' from deep inside. We're just movin' around and actin' on the surface. Then we've cheated the wirin' at its deepest level. Then we can eat and sleep and fuck and preserve ourselves with the smallest amount of energy possible. 'Cause the heart of our energy will be bound up with the real. And that's when we'll experience true and lastin' happiness."

Ray sighed. "So what do we do? How do we make a living?"

"Just go about doin' good things for people. Be a servant. You want to fix transmissions with me? You can do that. I got plenty of work. And, hell, we're doin' a good service. We're helpin' people get around in a safe vehicle."

Ray pondered the offer. He wasn't much good with mechanical things. *Ah, what the hell?* "Sure, I'll help you out. Thanks."

Aaron swallowed the last of his ale. "I got somethin' else to ask you. You want to help Maddy and me start a Peacemaker Order?"

"What's a Peacemaker Order?"

"It's an organization that promotes peaceful, sane livin'. It's all based on what we've been discussin' tonight. It's about doin' good and helpin' folks."

Ray smiled wide and blinked his eyes. He felt a heaviness in his chest fall away. "That sounds just fine to me."

Aaron nodded. He reached out his long, burly arm and wrapped it around Ray's shoulder with brotherly warmth. The two wayfarers of life stared into the glassy reflections of the back bar with a lightness of being that was more than bearable.

Chapter 69

The old monk leaned through the open window of the cab and gently patted Alexander on the shoulder. Motioning the driver to depart, he stepped back off the dirt road outside the Goa Gajah temple and watched the cab drive off into shrouds of billowing dust. His gaze followed his lowering arm and beheld his rotting sandals with a look of happy indifference. The holy man walked into the temple courtyard where twenty or thirty devotees were waiting for him to give his daily satsang. He sat in a wicker chair under a small canvas canopy and composed himself. He closed his eyes and breathed deeply for a few moments and then opened his eyes with a composure that suggested some deep, placid residence from which he viewed the temporal realm.

With hands placed together, he subtly bowed to his followers. "Alexander is going home. It is as necessary that he leave us as it was necessary that he join us. Everything that happens is necessary. Otherwise, it would not happen. It does not matter whether we like what happens. Life has its own reasons. It does not care what we like or dislike. That is why it is best to accept whatever happens with happy indifference and just do whatever we can to make the world a better place." The old monk raised his eyebrows and looked out over the congregation with prescient stillness. "Sometimes we do not know what to do to make the world a better place. We are at a loss. That too is okay. That too is necessary." The monk smiled gently, his gray eyes moist and searching. "Maybe sometimes it is best to do nothing. Maybe sometimes it is best to remain still and let the world work itself out without our interference." The monk looked up at the still, blue sky as if expecting something to fall from the heavens. "One of the last *Upanishads* tells the story of a group of spiritual seekers sitting at the feet of the guru. With exasperation, they tell the guru that they have done all the practices; they have chanted all the mantrams; they have performed all the rituals; and yet they are still unenlightened. 'Master, what are we to do now?' they ask. The master closes his eyes and sits motionless for a long time. Then he says, 'Be quiet.' That's it. Be quiet." The old monk cast his graceful glance upon the congregation and shook his head. "Life is strange. We exhaust ourselves trying to do what we think is right or proper or good. And it never seems to work out. And then one day, we stop trying. We just become still and quiet. Then we just do what we do. Simply. Peacefully. With gratitude." The monk smiled. "That is enlightenment."

The congregation sat quietly, staring at the old monk with expectation. They wanted more. They always wanted more. The old monk slowly got up and walked away. As he walked toward his hut, he heard wind chimes tinkling in the distance. *Just so,* he thought. *Just so.*

Chapter 70

~ *One Month Later* ~

Raymond Lessing sat on the deck of his post-and-beam farmhouse overlooking the wooded landscape below. The trees swayed gently in the breeze and painted green the temporal realm. The afternoon sun was warm on his neck and arms, and the frosty glass of lemonade, which he held in his left hand, radiated a spiral of welcome coolness up his arm. He turned his head and looked at Alex sitting beside him. Alex. Alex who was wrapped in the baby blue cotton blanket. Alex who shivered spasmodically every minute or so. Alex who needed assistance cleaning away the spittle that occasionally pooled at the corners of his mouth.

Alex raised his eyes in recognition. "You worried about me, Ray?" His voice was as thin and shallow as a whisper.

"No. Not really. Considering what you've been through, I think you're doing fine."

"What have I been through?"

Ray smiled compassionately. "You've been away, Alex. On a journey. It's taken its toll, and now you're recovering."

Alex shivered and pulled his blanket tight. "Did I find what I was looking for?"

"I don't know. Maybe. What do you think?"

"Maybe. Maybe I found it and didn't much like it. And that's why I'm sitting here like a zombie."

Ray chuckled. "Zombies can't think. They can't talk. You're not a zombie."

Alex smiled strangely. "I guess you're right." Alex stared out at the green leaves dancing in the treetops. "Who am I, Ray?"

"I don't know." Ray took a deep, happy breath. "Who am I, Alex?"

"Don't know."

Ray smiled and nodded. "Then I'd say we're even."

Chapter 71

~ One Month Later ~

September 11, 2001 – 9:45 a.m.

Aaron Riley sat on the bed and placed his hand gently on Maddy's cheek. She slept soundly, and Aaron thought she looked like some kind of angel that had been mysteriously abandoned within the earthly realm. "Maddy. Maddy. Wake up."

Maddy fought to open her eyes. They were glued shut by deep sleep. "What? What's up?"

"You've gotta see this. On TV. You've gotta see this."

"I don't want to watch TV." Maddy groaned and rolled away from him.

"Please, Maddy. I'm serious."

In the persistent fog of sleep, Maddy heard in Aaron's voice a plea that she did not recognize. It claimed her attention, and she sat up. "What's happened?"

Aaron's face was pale and sorrowful. "We've been attacked."

"What?"

"We've been attacked. In New York City. By terrorists."

"Oh, my God. How bad is it?"

"It's bad. Two planes have flown into the World Trade Center. New York City is paralyzed. People are runnin' in the streets, screamin'." Aaron's eyes were clear and strong behind his pained frown. "This breaks my heart, Maddy. It just breaks my heart."

Maddy took Aaron's head in her hands and brought it to her breast.

~ ~ ~ ~ ~

10:02 a.m.

Frank and Barbara-Jean were driving southeast on Route 281. Frank had just bought a used Mercury Cougar, and he and Barbara-Jean were giving it a spin, heading toward the sleepy Pennsylvania town of Somerset under a glorious canopy of blue sky and sunshine. They had planned this little getaway sometime back and were happy that their plans had finally materialized. They had just passed the cutoff to Shanksville and were gleefully singing Motown tunes at the top of their lungs. Frank had bought a new radio for the car but hadn't found time to install it, so the singing just came kind of naturally.

They really never had a chance. Time stopped with the black, thunderous scream of the engines just above them. The explosive vibrations from the twisting, plunging aircraft blew the car off the road and into oblivion.

~ ~ ~ ~ ~

10:03 a.m.

Ray hung up the phone and slowly walked back to his chair on the farmhouse deck. He sat down and stared into the soft blue sky hovering above the plethora of trees that graced his personal expanse of wilderness. He heard the birds singing nature's sweet symphony in harmonies that were not rightfully of this world. So peaceful. So sublime. So completely incongruous.

He turned to Alex. "That was Aaron on the phone."

Alex turned in his chair and looked at Ray through lazy, glazed eyes. His unshaven face gave him the countenance of a madman. "How's old Aaron doing these days?"

"Aaron's fine." Ray contemplated going no further but decided to continue on. "He called to tell me about a tragedy that has just occurred."

"A tragedy? As in Shakespeare?"

Ray was momentarily taken back by the comment but then considered it. "Yeah. As in Shakespeare."

"Which play?"

"This play has yet to be written."

Alex screwed up his face in rarefied contemplation. Then he sat quiet for a few moments. Then he spoke. "Or maybe the play has already been written, but no one's read it yet." A long silence. "Or maybe it's a play that no one is capable of reading. Perhaps we don't have the mental constructs within which to frame it."

Ray squinted and studied Alex closely. He could have sworn that Alex's eyes had cleared and that there was a twinkle in them that spoke of some rare and hidden knowledge.

"Ray?"

"Yes."

"Are you going to send me away?"

"No."

"I wouldn't blame you."

"I'm not sending you anywhere."

Alex suggestively raised his eyebrows. "Not even to Dr. Bevis?"

Ray laughed at the thought. "You're staying here with me, Alex."

Alex nodded and turned away.

Ray thought about the tragedy in New York and decided to go inside and watch the news. He got up, gently patted Alex on the shoulder, and walked into the house.

Alex turned his head skyward and sighted a bald eagle high in the trees above him. He watched the mighty bird look down upon him as if it were eavesdropping. Alex nodded with satisfaction that it might be the case and turned his head down and studied his hands. His hands looked familiar to him. Like some part of himself he could depend upon. He took a deep breath and exhaled with an uncanny acceptance and a prescient stillness that made him feel as if he were part of something far grander than himself.

Printed in the United States
134991LV00001B/149/P